2020
(2)

*Two are better than
one....For if they fall, the
one will lift up his fellow.*

–*Ecclesiastes* 4:9–10 (KJV)

MYSTERIES *of* LANCASTER COUNTY

Another's Treasure
Garage Sale Secret

GARAGE SALE SECRET

MYSTERIES *of* LANCASTER COUNTY

Elizabeth Ludwig

New York

CHAPTER ONE

Mary Classen Baxter lifted her face to the sky and let the rising sun's rays warm her skin. Still hard to believe, but here she was on the farm where she grew up. After so many years away, she was finally adjusting to living back in Bird-in-Hand. She'd been back three months now, and truth be told, it wasn't so bad. Mary sighed in contentment and flicked away a persistent fly that appeared determined to land on her nose. She relished the slower pace she'd had in her old life in Indianapolis, the fresh air, and the camaraderie flourishing between herself and her sisters. She was even getting used to Reddy's gentle nudge prying her from sleep.

As if on cue, the family rooster crowed, breaking the early morning silence.

"You're too late, Reddy," she called, cupping her hand to her mouth. "I'm awake."

Reddy's raucous song flowed on, uninterrupted. Mary smiled. The old bird would soon have everyone in the house up and moving. Her dachshund, Tinkerbelle, or Tink, as she affectionately called her, didn't much care for Reddy. She lifted her head and sent a low growl in the direction of the barn.

"Crazy rooster. Good thing I've already put the coffee on, huh?" she said, reaching down to rub Tink behind the ears.

Tink gazed up at her, her tail thumping the porch. Stretching one last time, Mary turned and pulled open the screen door, its grumpy screech adding harmony to Reddy's chorus. From the rear of the house, pots and pans clattered. Apparently, Martha was up before the old rooster's alarm too.

Mary laid the morning newspaper on the hall table and stopped to take a deep breath in through her nose. Was that bacon she smelled? She changed into her house slippers and headed for the kitchen with her mouth watering.

Martha eyed her over the pancake batter she was whisking. "You're up early."

Mary pulled a coffee cup from the cupboard. "I have an errand I need to run before church, so I gave myself a little extra time to get the animals fed and watered."

The pancake batter hissed as it hit the griddle. Somehow, Martha always managed to get her pancakes perfectly round, a trick Mary had never mastered. Not that she had need of the skill now, with Martha's excellent cooking keeping them all fed.

"Are you going to the cemetery after the service?" Martha set the batter bowl aside and reached for a spatula. She jabbed it toward a platter of bacon. "Get yourself a slice."

Mary happily obliged. She bit off a piece and chewed it. "Yeah, I thought I would stop by. Hey, do you suppose that old caretaker—what was his name—still works there?"

"Duffy Porter?" Martha waited a moment and then deftly flipped the pancake. "No idea. Why?"

"I was thinking about planting a dogwood and maybe setting a little bench next to it, but I don't know what the rules are regarding that type of thing. I thought I would check with him first."

Martha put a finished pancake on the platter with the others. "You've always loved visiting that cemetery, even before we laid Daddy and now Mama to rest there."

Mary finished off the bacon, then wiped her hands on a paper towel. "It's so peaceful and calm there. The wind rustles through the trees...the setting is beautiful and perfect for painting...I like it."

Spying Martha's grimace, Mary chuckled. She and her sisters were alike in many ways, but this was definitely not one of them. She grabbed three plates from the cupboard and set them next to the griddle, then went to the refrigerator for the butter. She set it and a knife next to the plates before turning toward the pantry.

"Hey, do we have any more of that all-natural maple syrup Lizzie bought from the craft fair?"

"Second shelf," Martha called.

Mary found it and carried it back to the counter where Martha had two steaming pancakes waiting on a plate.

She pushed the plate toward Mary and slid two more pancakes onto the second plate for herself. "So what time do you think you'll be back from the cemetery? I heard there was a large estate sale over near New Holland. I was thinking about going."

Estate sales were fun, but Mary shook her head and pointed to the satchel hanging on a hook next to the door. "Probably better go without me. I was thinking of taking my paintbrushes."

Martha sighed, and Mary knew why. Used to be she'd lose all track of time when she was sitting in front of an easel. Granted, it had been a long time since she'd devoted herself to her art, but she was hoping it would be that way again once she got a little paint on her fingers.

She gobbled her breakfast, poured a second cup of coffee in an insulated travel mug, picked up her satchel, and headed toward the door.

"Mary?"

Mary hiked the satchel strap higher and looked over her shoulder at Martha, who pointed at Mary's feet. "Your shoes."

"What? Oh." Mary looked down with a giggle and wiggled her toes. She was still wearing her slippers. "Guess I should change, huh?"

Her sister's laughter echoing in her ears, Mary dashed up the stairs to her closet, shoved her feet into a sturdy pair of boots, and then continued on her way. She made a quick stop for gas and a birthday card for her Sunday school teacher before heading to church. Thankfully, the early service was a lot more relaxed than the traditional one that took place after. Her boots and casual slacks were not out of place there.

After the service concluded, she slipped away from the people lingering and chatting in the foyer and headed for the cemetery. A light breeze rustled through the leaves on the trees as she exited her car and wound down the narrow path toward her parents' graves. Instantly, a sense of peace lifted her spirits. Granted, it *was* mingled with a tiny bit of sorrow and a smidgeon of loneliness for her father's full laugh and her mother's gentle wisdom, but it was peace nonetheless.

She slowed as she passed a row of grave markers bearing familiar names. There was a stone for her old high school English teacher and one for a former pastor of their church. Farther down were two identical stones for the twin boys who had died one summer in a boating accident when Mary was a teenager. There was even an elegant marble stone for Wavel Hebert, the curmudgeonly owner of the diner where Mary used to drink root beer floats and chat with her friends—that was, when old Wavel wasn't chasing them out. She smiled. That was the thing about small towns. Everyone knew everyone.

Finally, she reached her parents' graves, and her eyes filled with tears at the words etched into the headstone.

Beloved Father and Mother.

Yes, they were beloved as parents, but they were so much more. Mentors. Friends. Cheerleaders. Even during the rough spots.

"It doesn't matter how old you are, when your parents pass away, you still feel like an orphan."

Her father's words struck a poignant chord in Mary's heart. Her father had whispered them at Grandma Lois's funeral nearly a decade ago, but Mary remembered it as though he'd spoken them yesterday.

"You were right, Daddy," she whispered, running her hand over the name etched into the marble. "I do feel like an orphan sometimes."

Nearby, a bird's chirrup drew her from her melancholy. He lit on a large black headstone, eyed her for a moment with his little blue head cocked to one side, and then set about preening. Apparently he didn't view her as a threat.

Mary smiled, slid her phone carefully from her pocket, and snapped a quick picture to study later. Disturbed by the sound, her feathered friend chirped his displeasure before fluttering off in a flurry of wings. Ah, well. At least she'd have the picture.

She enlarged the photo, glad to see she'd captured a crisp likeness. Oftentimes, her attempts at phone photography came out blurry. Still, carrying a phone was a lot easier than lugging a three-pound Polaroid around her neck.

Enlarging the photo had the added benefit of enlarging the name carved into the headstone. Mary frowned. Paul Classen. Uncle Paul. She looked up at the marker and then back down at her phone. She'd forgotten he was buried up there. Suddenly, it struck her as really sad and lonely.

Leaving the cluster of family markers, Mary struck up the sloping hill toward his grave. When she reached it, she paused to catch her breath, her hands braced firmly on her hips.

She looked back downhill. "That was quite a hike."

And why? It really was odd that he was buried so far from the rest of the family. If she'd been told the reason why, it escaped her now.

"At least the view from up here is beautiful, eh, Uncle Paul?"

She rested her hand atop his tombstone. Below them, acres of rich farmland stretched to the farthest corners of Lancaster County. In the distance, pale white silos poked at the sky.

She sighed happily and pulled her satchel off her shoulder. This would be a perfect spot to get her creative juices flowing. She lowered herself to the ground, took out her brushes and a few tubes of paint, and got to work. Before long, she'd lost herself in the almost hypnotic strokes of her brush across the canvas.

"Pretty."

Mary jumped and let out a small shriek. The movement sent her hand skittering upward, creating an ugly dark slash across her otherwise lovely painting. She stared at it in dismay.

"Ooh...sorry about that. I didn't mean to startle you." The owner of the voice smiled, exposing deep dimples on either side of his mouth.

"Th—that's all right," Mary stammered as she collected her paints and threw them into her satchel. "I was concentrating and didn't hear you walk up."

The man watched her with a remorseful frown. "I hope you're not leaving because of me." He hefted a rake in one hand. "I've got to get back to work. I just noticed you up here painting and...well..."

He shrugged shyly and waved his hand at the area surrounding them. Mary followed his gaze. Obviously, he'd been working in a wide circle around her for some time. Piles of branches, grass clippings, and debris lay scattered about. No doubt he'd been wondering when, if ever, she'd be finished.

"I'm so sorry." Mary stood and threw the rest of her belongings into her bag and tossed the strap over her shoulder. "I was completely absorbed in my painting. I get like that when I'm working."

"Me too." He chuckled and stuck out his hand. "Name's Rafe Porter."

Mary gave his hand a shake. He had a strong grip, but his palms weren't nearly as calloused as she might have expected from a gardener. And why was he working on a Sunday, anyway? Too shy to ask, she pulled her hand away and crossed her arms. "Mary Baxter."

He leaned his arms atop his rake. "I don't think I've met you before. Are you from around here, Mary Baxter?"

She nodded. "I grew up here. My name used to be Classen."

He straightened, and his gaze fell to Uncle Paul's headstone. "Classen, as in..."

"He was my uncle."

"Really?" His eyes gleamed with genuine interest. "So then, maybe *you* could tell me why Paul Classen is buried way up here when all the other Classens are down there." He inclined his head down the hill. "I've always wondered about it."

She shrugged and grinned wryly. "You'll have to keep wondering, I'm afraid. It's a mystery, even to me. My uncle died before I was born."

His wiggled his eyebrows. "I love a good mystery."

What could she say to that? Mary nodded lamely. "Me too." She gripped the strap on her satchel tightly. "So, Porter, huh? Any relation to Duffy Porter?"

"He's my uncle." Rafe gestured around the cemetery. "I know it's Sunday, but I had the afternoon free, so I figured I'd come by. I try to give Uncle Duffy a hand now and then, whenever he complains that his sciatica is giving him trouble."

So he didn't actually work here. That explained his nice hands. Just *hands*, she corrected quickly. Whether they were nice or not was irrelevant.

Their eyes met, and worried he might see her thoughts reflected there, Mary pointed toward the far corner of the cemetery where the caretaker's cottage was located. "Well, it's been some time since I've seen your uncle, but from what I remember, you certainly look like him. I remember him smiling a lot and…" She motioned rather bashfully toward Rafe's thick salt-and-pepper locks. "He had good hair."

Good hair? Good grief! She stifled a groan.

He laughed then—a rich, deep sound that invited her to smile with him.

He bent and retrieved her painting, lingering over it a moment before he gave it to her. "So you're a painter, huh?"

Her face warmed. She took the painting gingerly so as not to smudge the paint not already marred by the slash of brown. "It's a hobby. I'm just now getting back into it."

"Really? You're good. I would have thought you did it professionally."

More heat crept up her neck. "Thank you."

He pointed to the canvas. "I'm really sorry about messing you up. Can you fix it?"

"I can try. I'll have to look at it again when I get home."

He nodded. "I hope so. It's really beautiful. And the mark almost looks like a person standing there looking out over the view."

Mary's gaze dropped to the painting. Indeed, she could almost imagine it as he described. And from here, the vantage would be her uncle's. Melancholy took hold of her as she imagined him standing in this very spot, looking down over the family plots—alone. Isolated. Lonely. Why hadn't she ever bothered to find out what happened?

"Oops. I've lost you."

She blinked and drew her gaze back to Rafe. "Sorry."

He lifted one hand. "Nope, I interrupted you. No need to apologize. I should be getting back to work anyway."

He lingered despite his words, a look of curiosity on his handsome face.

Again, with the adjectives!

Mary squeezed the strap on her satchel as her thoughts winged to Bill Richmond, an old friend she'd reconnected with here. "Well, it was nice meeting you, Rafe. Please tell your uncle hello for me."

"Will do." He shifted the rake to his other hand, and a smile stretched his lips. "It was nice meeting you too, Mary."

Mary turned and hurried down the hill. *Crumbs.* What was it about Rafe Porter that set her on edge? She hadn't felt this way since—

She shuddered as she reached her car and tossed her satchel inside. Of course she remembered the last time she'd felt this way. It had turned out to be a complete disaster, and she had vowed never, ever, to let herself feel that way again.

CHAPTER TWO

Monday morning dawned bright and beautiful—a perfect day for creative inspiration. Mary added one last dab of paint to the shadowy figure overlooking the cemetery and then sidestepped around Tink to examine her work. She tilted her head to the side and closed one eye. This wasn't nearly as intricate as some of her old paintings, but she figured she'd work her way up once she got back into the swing of things.

Finally, she blew out a breath. Tink lifted her head and stared up at Mary, her little nose twitching.

Mary twisted the easel for her to see. "What do you think, Tink? It's perfect, right?"

"What's perfect?" The screen door banged shut, and her eldest sister, Elizabeth, stepped out onto the porch, a glass of lemonade in her hand. Her gaze traveled to the painting. "Ooh, did you finish it?"

Mary set her paintbrush down in the easel tray and reached for a towel to wipe the paint from her hands. "I think I'm finally satisfied with it. What do you think?"

Elizabeth stepped closer and handed the glass to Mary. "Here, I brought you this."

Mary took the lemonade, and Elizabeth crossed her arms to study the painting. While she waited, Mary took a sip from the glass. The sweet-yet-tart taste puckered her lips.

Finally, when she couldn't stand the tension any longer, she set her glass on the porch railing and propped her hands on her hips. "Well? Don't keep me in suspense. What do you think?"

Elizabeth turned to her, eyes wide. "I'd forgotten how good you are."

Mary's shoulders sagged with relief. "Really?"

Elizabeth nodded and slipped her arm around Mary's waist. "It's beautiful. It makes me feel...well...it makes me *feel.*" She shrugged and turned apologetic eyes toward Mary. "I can't explain it."

Mary sighed with pleasure. "You don't have to. I get it. I felt the same way painting it."

Elizabeth looked back at the painting. "The man?"

"Uncle Paul." Mary pulled back to look at her sister. "Lizzie, why wasn't he buried with the family? Do you remember?"

Elizabeth shook her head and tucked a bit of hair behind her ear to keep the wind from blowing it into her eyes. "It was too long ago. I remember there being something of a scandal though."

Mary lifted her brows. "A scandal?"

"Yep. Remember? People always got quiet anytime Uncle Paul's name was mentioned around us kids."

"Hmm."

Mary tapped her chin while Elizabeth moved to one of the rocking chairs. The old seat creaked as she sat.

"So? What are you going to do with it?" she asked.

"The painting?" Mary began gathering up her paintbrushes, Rafe Porter's words ringing in her ears. "I was kind of thinking about trying to sell it...you know...if it's good enough."

"It's definitely good enough."

Mary paused, then dropped the brushes into a cup of clean water. "You think so?"

"Of course. You've always had such a keen eye." Elizabeth gave the rocking chair a push with her toe, creating a bumping rhythm against the wooden slats of the porch floor.

"Thanks, Lizzie." Mary picked up the painting and held it at arm's length. It *was* good, better than she'd expected after all these years. "I, um, I was kind of thinking of hanging it in the shop."

The screen door screeched again. This time, it was Martha stepping out with the family's border collie, Pal, who zipped off across the lawn with Tink in hot pursuit. Martha waved a dishrag at them then set a basket of damp laundry on the porch.

"You don't have to line dry those, you know," Elizabeth said.

"I know, but I like the way the fresh air makes them smell." Martha turned to Mary. "What were you thinking of hanging in the shop?"

Mary replaced the painting on the easel and stepped back to show her sister. Martha oohed in appreciation. "Wow. That turned out really beautiful." She paused and pointed to the figure depicted in the painting. "Who's that?"

"It's Uncle Paul." Elizabeth spoke before Mary could, a note of worry in her voice. Creases deepened on her brow, and her fingers plucked nervously at her bottom lip.

Mary braced herself as Martha's gaze swung to fasten on her. "You painted Uncle Paul?"

"Well, a representation of him," she explained quickly. "It struck me yesterday as kind of sad that he's buried all alone up there on the hill, away from the rest of the family. And then Rafe Porter stopped by—"

"Duffy Porter's nephew?" Martha frowned. "I remember him. I didn't know he was back in town."

"You knew him?" Mary asked.

"Well, I knew of him." Martha glanced at Elizabeth. "Didn't you go to school with him?"

She nodded. "He was a year younger than me." She looked at Mary. "Anyway, he stopped by? Was he there visiting a grave?"

"Actually, he was helping out his uncle at the cemetery."

"So, apparently, Duffy's still the caretaker, eh?" Martha said. "Did you ask about the dogwood?"

"I didn't get a chance. Rafe was the only one there. He said his uncle's sciatica was giving him trouble, and he had the afternoon free, so he went by to help out. When I introduced myself, he asked about Uncle Paul's grave, which is what started me wondering."

Elizabeth glanced at Martha. "Do *you* remember why Uncle Paul wasn't buried with the family?"

Martha shook her head and leaned against the railing. "That was a long time ago. I do remember he was always sort of a black sheep." She held up her finger. "Oh, and wasn't there something about a disagreement between him and some other members of the family?"

"Yes, if I remember correctly." Elizabeth clasped her hands in her lap. "Mary is thinking about selling the painting in the shop."

Martha's gaze drifted to the painting. "It certainly is beautiful…"

The same note of doubt Mary had heard in Elizabeth's voice crept into Martha's.

"But...? What is it?" Mary asked.

Martha said nothing for a moment, then pressed her lips together tightly and shook her head. "It's nothing. The store is just as much yours as it is ours. You have every right to display anything you wish."

"Thank you for that," Mary said quietly. Her gaze bounced from Martha to Elizabeth. "But you're still worried about something. I can hear it in your voices."

Elizabeth pressed a hand to her chin, her eyes troubled. Whatever it was, she and Martha were apparently on the same page. They shared a long look. Finally, Elizabeth spoke.

"It's just...we're a little concerned about what the rest of the family will say. Shouldn't we figure out what happened between them and Uncle Paul first?"

Mary thought a moment and then glanced at the painting in disappointment. She could see Elizabeth's point. Even if their immediate Classen relatives didn't see the painting themselves, there was a very active grapevine that would let them know what was hanging in Grandma Lois's shop. The situation with Uncle Paul must have been a very sticky topic.

She swallowed hard and lifted her chin. "You're right. I certainly don't want to upset anyone. I don't have to display this one. I can paint something else."

A moment of awkward silence followed, broken only by Tink's panting as she scurried back up onto the porch to flop at Mary's feet, and the lazy calls of a flock of barn swallows.

"Then again…" Martha rubbed her chin thoughtfully. "We wouldn't have to say it's a painting of Uncle Paul?"

Her voice lifted as if in question as she looked from Elizabeth to Mary.

Elizabeth rose to stand next to Mary. "That's true. We could just put it up for sale and say nothing more about it."

Mary gulped down a sudden knot. "Do you really think anyone would be interested in buying it?"

"Of course." Elizabeth placed her arm around Mary's shoulders. "You have a wonderful talent, Mary. You won't have any trouble selling it. I have no doubt."

Martha agreed. "And it might be nice to have a few pieces of reasonably priced local art in the barn. I can see it being a big draw."

A bit of the tension eased from Mary's chest. Her sisters weren't trying to discourage her. They were just concerned about how the other members of their family might feel.

Elizabeth gave Mary's shoulder a squeeze. "It's a beautiful painting, and it deserves to be displayed. Don't you agree, Martha?" She thrust out her chin and stared at Martha expectantly.

To Mary's relief, Martha pushed off the railing and nodded. "It's beautiful. And it will motivate us to do something we should have done a long time ago—find out what happened with Uncle Paul."

Hope flickered inside Mary's chest. "Really?"

"Really." Elizabeth dropped her arm from about Mary's shoulders and hitched her thumb toward the barn. "I was just about to head that way so I could get started restocking some of the inventory. Why don't we go and find a place for it now before the store opens? I think I know the perfect spot."

Mary hesitated. She appreciated her sisters' support, but she didn't want them to feel obligated. "Are you sure? There's no hurry to hang it now."

"Now's as good a time as any." Martha reached down for the laundry basket and propped it on her hip. "I'll just hang these towels and then meet you two down at the store."

"Nah." Mary took the basket from her sister with a grin. "We'll all help. It'll get done quicker that way."

With the three of them helping, the task only took a few minutes. Mary set the empty basket on the porch stairs and then followed her sisters down to the old barn her great-grand-parents had converted into a secondhand resale shop they named Secondhand Blessings. The hand-painted sign creaked as the sisters moved to unlock the door.

Martha jabbed her thumb upward. "Say, Mary, maybe you could give the sign a new coat of paint, seeing as you're back into that now."

"Martha, it isn't the same thing," Elizabeth said, withdrawing a key from the pocket of her skirt and inserting it into the lock.

Martha's chin jutted stubbornly. "I know, but you keep saying you're going to hire somebody to do it, and Mary could easily do as good a job or better. Why not let her?" She turned her gaze to Mary. "Well?"

"I'll be happy to do it," Mary said, mostly to soothe Elizabeth but also because Martha could be as tenacious as a bulldog when she got an idea in her head. Mary laid her painting carefully on the counter and then crossed to the light switch and turned on the overheads. A low hum split the air as they flickered to life. "Martha, didn't you say you were thinking about going to an estate sale in New Holland yesterday?"

Martha shook her head. "It was a bust. A lot of nice stuff, but nothing I thought would sell well in the store."

"Hmm, that's too bad." Actually, it only justified Mary's decision not to go, but she didn't say so. Martha was always thinking about the store and looking to add inventory, even on her days off.

Mary moved back to the counter and eyed a spot high up on the wall just to the left of the cash register. "Say, what about hanging the painting there?"

"It is sort of bare," Elizabeth agreed, bracing her hands on her hips. She looked over her shoulder at Martha. "What do you think?"

"I was thinking about the wall above the bookshelves, but we certainly could use something to brighten up this wall." She shrugged and then turned back to the task of getting the store ready to open.

Mary sighed with relief. That had gone much easier than she expected after seeing her sisters' hesitation that morning. She went to fetch a ladder and a nail and soon had the canvas on proud display. After asking for Elizabeth's help to straighten the picture, Mary took a moment to look around. *Warm, bright, inviting* were the words that came to mind as she surveyed the shop. There were large open areas, with beautiful handcrafted and antique furniture, as well as row upon row of Amish-made oak shelving filled with one-of-a-kind items just waiting for the right customer to come along. In another open area was a colorful alphabet rug with small tables and chairs for children. Mary made sure there were always plenty of crayons, drawing tablets, books, and wooden toys to keep them occupied while their parents shopped. Along one wall was Martha's display case—replacing the earlier table—bulging with artfully arranged baked goods and, when in season, jars of homemade jams, honey, and maple syrup. They had discussed having lemonade available to their customers in the summer and hot apple cider in the winter, but since it was only May, they didn't have to make that decision just yet.

Amish quilts, needlecraft pictures and samplers, and inspirational wooden etchings adorned the walls. Mary's eyes fell on one of her favorites: "I thank God for protecting me from what I thought I wanted and blessing me with what I didn't know I needed." She once again breathed a prayer of gratitude for new beginnings and this place of roots and stability.

She climbed carefully down from the ladder and set about helping Elizabeth with the restocking. Soon, it was time to open, and their first customers shuffled into the store. Among them were four of their regulars, Della Bradford, Nancy VanSlyke, Beverly Stout, and Linda Martin. All four women were avid garage and estate sale mavens and often brought in quality items to sell on consignment. Mary rushed over to see what treasures they'd discovered this week.

She smiled brightly. "Good morning, ladies."

"Morning, Mary," they chimed in response.

Nancy waved eagerly. "You'll never guess what we found. Come see."

While Nancy unpacked the box, Beverly chattered on and on about how it had been her idea to peruse the sale ads in the local newspaper and how she had stumbled upon an interesting listing for a garage sale and insisted they go.

"We really did find some great antiques," Linda said, taking one of the items Nancy handed her and unwrapping it gingerly. "Ooh, this is one of the Wedgwood plates I bought. Isn't it lovely?"

Mary traced the delicate, scrolled edge appreciatively. "It really is, Linda. Is there more than just this piece?"

"Uh-huh. An entire place setting, and not a chip on any of them. I'll show you."

She bent and took the wrapped pieces from the box. While she unpacked them, Della held up an antique silver teapot with graceful gadrooned lines. Mary gasped when she saw it. The spout curved in an S-shape and a quince finial adorned the lid, but it was the unusual, ear-shaped handle that caught her eye.

"Della, that is beautiful."

She beamed proudly. "You think so? Nancy said I paid too much for it, but I couldn't resist. It's just so lovely, I was tempted to keep it for myself."

"I can certainly understand why." Mary lifted the teapot high and examined the bottom. "There's a maker's mark." She licked her thumb and rubbed the etching gingerly and then studied it again. Satisfied, she handed the teapot back to Della. "I believe that's a Janus double head, but we'll have to ask Elizabeth to be certain. If so, you may have purchased yourself a pretty valuable piece of Belgian silver."

Della's eyes widened. "I'm surprised you know that." A flush deepened the color on her cheeks, and she reached out to clasp Mary's shoulder. "Oh, I'm sorry. That came out all wrong."

Mary stifled a guffaw, the result of which sounded like a snort. "Don't be sorry. I agree with you. Hanging around my sisters has definitely paid off."

Appeased, Della lowered her hand. "Well, I knew it was just too pretty to leave behind. I'm glad I bought it."

Linda patted her shoulder. "Good job, Della."

"Yes, really good." Mary touched the teapot again and rechecked the maker's mark. "This really is beautiful. I'm tempted...how much did you say you wanted for it?"

Della gave her an amount and waited. Mary did a quick mental calculation of her savings account and then nodded. "I'll take it."

"*You'll* take it?" Nancy's eyes rounded. "Didn't you want to check with Martha on the mark?"

"Some things are made valuable simply because they speak to your heart," Mary said, running her finger lovingly over the side of the teapot. "This is saying 'take me home.'"

The women laughed. Mary rewrapped the teapot and set it aside. "What else have you got?"

"Just a few other things. Those were the most exciting items," Della said. She unwrapped three lovely cups and saucers, gilt-edged and almost paper-thin. "I was hoping you could hang on to these for me and not put them out yet. The lady at the sale told me she thought she'd seen the fourth to this set but wasn't sure where she'd put it. I'd like to sell them all together."

"That won't be a problem at all." Mary picked up a saucer and admired the delicate blush-pink roses circling the edge. "When do you think you'll know?"

Della began rewrapping the cups. "She told me she'd have time to look later today. I'll either bring the other place setting by tomorrow, or call you and let you know to go ahead and sell them separately."

Mary nodded. "That'll be just fine. I'll take you over to Martha so we can get the rest of this inventoried."

"Don't bother," Beverly said, waving to the people milling through the store. "We can do it. You go on and help your customers."

"Okay, thank you," Mary began, but Beverly was already hefting the box and leading the others toward the bakery display case where Martha was working. Mary turned and nearly bumped into Della, who was standing with her head tilted back, staring up at Mary's painting.

She pointed. "That's new."

Mary swallowed nervously. "Yes, I just finished it."

Della's mouth dropped open. *"You* painted that? I didn't know you were an artist."

Mary nodded, her cheeks warming under Della's stare. "I used to do quite a bit of painting in my younger days, actually. I'm getting back into it now that I have some free time."

Della directed her gaze upward again. "You should. You're talented." Her lips puckered. "It's missing something though."

"Missing something?" Mary crossed to stand next to her and stared up at her painting. "Do you mean the colors?"

Della laid her finger alongside her chin. "No, the colors are fine, but it needs a frame to really set it off."

"Oh, I know," Mary said quickly. "I left it unframed because a lot of times people want to choose something that matches their furnishings."

"Hmm. I suppose." Della squinted harder, and then the lines cleared from her brow, and she snapped her fingers. "I know that spot. That's the cemetery, isn't it?"

Mary's smile broadened, pleased that she'd managed to capture the setting so accurately as to have someone recognize it so easily. "Yes, that's the hill overlooking the Classen family plot."

"Interesting. Would you mind if I take a closer look?"

"Not at all," Mary said, hitching her thumb toward the stockroom. "Just let me fetch a ladder."

"I'll get it."

Startled by the masculine voice at her shoulder, Mary spun and was immediately transfixed by a brilliant smile and a familiar set of dimples.

"Rafe Porter." Mary fumbled behind her blindly for Della's hand and yanked her forward. "This is my friend Della Bradford."

Della stuck out her hand. "Rafe, huh? Are you Duffy Porter's nephew? I heard you were in town."

"The same. I'm here visiting for a few weeks." He shook her hand and then turned to Mary. "So, the ladder?"

She jumped as though she'd been poked. "Thank you, but it's really no bother."

He grinned at her. "I'm happy to help. Lead the way."

Hesitating any longer would appear rude. She motioned toward the stockroom. "Right this way."

Word of mouth about the store's reopening had been spreading around Bird-in-Hand and the surrounding area. Mary had to weave through customers on her way to the stockroom. She eyed Rafe over her shoulder. "You really don't have to help me. I put the picture up myself this morning. I'm sure I can get it down on my own."

He held up his hand. "I'm sure you can, but please, let me help."

She pushed open the stockroom door, turned on the light, and pointed toward the back wall. "The ladder is over there."

"Got it." Rafe eased past her and hoisted the ladder onto his shoulder. "All set."

Mary stepped aside to let him pass, then flicked off the light and closed the door. What was it with this Rafe Porter, anyway? Why was he so determined to help?

CHAPTER THREE

Rafe lowered the painting carefully into Mary's waiting hands. Clutching it tightly, she stepped back to let him step down off the ladder, then thanked him with a nod.

"That was nice. Thank you."

He waved his hand. "No problem. Should I put the ladder away?"

"I can do it. I wouldn't want to put you to any trouble."

He chuckled, a warm, full sound that had several people glancing their way.

"It's no trouble." To prove his point, he shouldered the ladder in one swift move and carried it away before she could say another word.

"Well, well." Della leaned in close to whisper in her ear. "He's certainly all grown up."

"You know him?"

"Knew him, when he was a kid, I mean. He looks very different now."

Mary swallowed and tore her eyes away. "I suppose. Anyway, here's the painting."

She carried it to a nearby table for Della to examine. Rafe Porter forgotten, Della removed a pair of reading glasses from her purse, perched them on her nose, and bent down close.

Her finger trailed the long figure on the hill. "This is such an interesting technique. Did you intend to paint the person in shadow?"

"Actually, that was an accident," Mary admitted.

"My fault," Rafe added, rejoining them. He shrugged and pushed his hands into the pockets of jeans. "I walked up on her while she was concentrating." He turned to Mary. "I'm glad you were able to make it into something nice. Your uncle Paul would be proud."

Mary froze. Hopefully, Della wouldn't notice—

"Uncle?" Della asked, her voice rising innocently.

Mortified, Mary glanced over her shoulder for a glimpse of her sisters. They were busy helping customers.

She turned back to Della. Fighting the queasiness rolling in her stomach, she said, "Yeah, um, the grave you see in the bottom left corner belongs to my uncle Paul. This shadow is him, looking over the graveyard."

"Paul Classen?" Della tilted her head to one side, thinking. "I remember that name."

"Really?" A flicker of excitement dispelled the unease. Mary moved closer and lowered her voice. "My sisters and I don't know all that much about him. He died before I was born, and Martha and Elizabeth were very young."

Della scratched her temple. "I can understand why you don't know much. That was all so long ago." She touched the shadow again. "An accident, huh? A bit of good luck, I'd say. It looks like it should have been there all along."

"I agree." Oblivious to the anxiety he'd caused, Rafe smiled broadly.

"Thank you. I'm happy with it." She shifted her weight to one foot and cleared her throat. "So, Della, what do you remember about my uncle Paul? Rafe asked me about him at the cemetery, and I was sorry to have to say that I really don't know that much about that part of the family's history."

Della scratched her head. Though she was older than Mary, she was still full of energy.

Her eyebrow rose. "He was your father's brother, right?"

"One of them," Mary said.

Della waved her hand. "Oh, yes. Everybody knew the Classen brood. There used to be a joke about them forming their own baseball team."

Mary laughed. "Yes, I remember hearing that a time or two. Uncle Paul was the youngest. My dad was closer to the middle."

"How old was Paul when he died?" Rafe asked.

Mary tilted her head, thinking. "Well, he and Daddy were only two years apart, and Daddy was twenty-nine when I was born, so I guess that must have made him about twenty-six or twenty-seven."

Della *tsk*ed sadly. "What a shame. If I remember right, it was a car accident that killed him, wasn't it?"

The words triggered a dim memory in Mary's brain, and she nodded. "Now that you mention it, I think I do remember hearing something like that."

She didn't add that what she'd heard had been discussed in quiet whispers and accompanied by sad shakes of the head.

Della fingered the edge of the painting. "Going back to your original question, to be honest, I don't remember much about Paul Classen, other than him being a very tall man. Of course, that could have been because I was only ten at the time." She laughed and smoothed a lock of hair behind her ear. "Everyone is tall to a ten-year-old."

Tall.

Mary tucked the detail away in her memory. She remembered pictures of her father's family. They were all tall, weren't they? The desire to find out more burned a little bit stronger inside her.

"Do you have any family members you could talk to?" Della asked. "Surely one of them would remember him."

"Yes, I could talk to them," Mary said, wondering which of her aunts and uncles would be less likely to berate her for asking.

A young man in a pair of designer jeans and wearing a blue sport coat ducked into Mary's view. He put his hand to his chest. "Excuse me. My name's Jim Olson. I couldn't help overhearing your conversation."

"Jim *Olson*?" Rafe's eyebrows rose, and he crossed his arms and stared.

"Yeah, I know," the young man said with a chuckle. "Like the character from the Superman comics." He turned to Mary. "You say you had an uncle named Paul Classen? My grandfather went to school with a man by that name."

Mary shot another quick glance around the store. So much for not drawing attention. Elizabeth and Martha were sure to give her a scolding when they found out. Fortunately, they were nowhere in sight. She swallowed hard and returned her gaze to the handsome young man peering earnestly at her. "Really?"

He nodded. "He and my grandfather were friends. Grandpa used to tell stories about the trouble he and a few others used to get into as kids. All good, clean fun," he amended quickly. "But did I hear you say your uncle passed away?"

Mary nodded. "Over fifty years ago, in fact."

He frowned. "Oh, that's too bad. I wonder if my grandpa knows about that."

His grandfather was still alive? Maybe he could tell her something about her uncle. Mary leaned forward. "You said your grandfather was friends with my uncle. Do you know if they stayed in touch after they graduated?"

He frowned. "I don't remember any recent stories of your uncle. I'd have to say they lost touch after high school. I guess now I know why." He paused a moment, then reached out to pat her arm. "I'm sorry."

"Thank you, but it's really all right. Like I said, I didn't know my uncle."

He removed his hand from her arm. "So did Paul Classen have any other family? A wife, kids, anything like that?"

Mary shook her head. "Unfortunately, no. He never married."

Jim hunched his shoulders. "Huh. That's too bad. But I guess that makes sense. If he had any surviving family, you could always talk to them about your uncle. Don't you have any other family you could talk to? Do they live in town?"

The conversation was quickly becoming uncomfortable. She looked to Della for help, but both she and Rafe seemed completely enthralled by the turn and were following the dialogue like spectators at a tennis match.

Mary crossed her arms. "Actually, we come from a pretty large family. I have several aunts and uncles."

Jim retreated a step and held up his hands. "Listen, I'm sorry. That was probably pretty nosy of me. I was just so curious when I heard you mention Paul Classen's name. Here recently, it seems like Grandpa talks more and more about the old days, so it kind of caught me off guard to hear that name from someone other than him."

Relax, Mary admonished herself silently. It wasn't his fault the conversation had gone awry. Rafe was the one who'd brought up Uncle Paul. She forced her stance to loosen and even managed a small smile. "No problem. I completely understand."

"Well, thanks for talking with me. It was a pleasure meeting the niece of Grandpa's old friend."

"You too."

Jim nodded to Della and Rafe and stuck out his hand. Mary shook it and then hesitated and motioned toward the painting.

"Listen, I don't suppose your grandfather would be interested in chatting with me about my uncle? I'd love to hear more about him."

He pulled a card from his pocket and gave it to her. "My number is on that card. Why don't you give me a couple of days to get in touch with my grandfather and then check back with me? I'm sure it will be no problem, since the one thing Grandpa loves to do most is to talk." He chuckled ruefully. "He never meets a stranger. He'll even strike up a conversation with people who dialed the wrong number."

Mary slipped his card into her jeans pocket. "My parents were the same way."

"Mine too," Della said.

Rafe nodded. "And Uncle Duffy. Must be that generation."

Mary looked back at Jim and shrugged. "Anyway, thank you for checking with him."

"No problem."

He waved his hand and ambled toward a display of old almanacs. Another customer was also perusing them, a woman of medium height and build with blond hair, slightly graying at the temples. She glanced at Jim Olson as he walked up and then moved aside to make room for him.

"Well, that was an interesting coincidence," Della said, gesturing toward Jim. She gave herself a small shake and turned back to the painting. "Anyway, let me know if you want me to scout out a frame. I'm pretty sure I could find something that fits."

Mary touched her finger to her lips, thought a moment, and then shook her head. "Thank you, Della, but I think I'd like to look through our basement first. There are lots of Grandma Lois's things down there, and I'm thinking maybe I can find something I can use."

Della patted her arm. "All right. I'll call or see you tomorrow and let you know what I find out about those cups."

"Thank you," Mary called after her, as Della drifted off to join the other ladies.

Rafe chimed in. "I'd probably better be going too. I promised Uncle Duffy I'd meet him for lunch. I just thought I'd check out your store before I headed that way."

"Actually, it's not my store," Mary said quickly. "My sisters and I own it together."

She looked around for them, but Martha was bent over a stack of used books, and Elizabeth was assisting a customer with a set of blue willow dishes. The door opened, sunlight glinting off the glass, and Mary was both glad and relieved to see Bill Richmond step through. When he spied her, a smile parted his lips, and he made a beeline toward them.

Rafe shifted to lean against the table. "Say, I don't suppose you'd care to join me for lunch?"

Lunch? Interest gleamed in Rafe's eyes, and a small smile lifted the corners of his mouth. Mary rubbed her palms against her pant legs and turned to greet Bill. Then she looked back at Rafe. "Thank you so much for the offer, but I need to stay here. We're busy today."

Rafe reached around her and extended his hand to Bill, who had stopped beside them. "Hello. Are you a friend of Mary's? I'm Rafe Porter."

Mary's cheeks warmed under Bill's curious gaze. No doubt he was wondering why she hadn't bothered to introduce them. He looked at Rafe, and the two shook hands.

"Bill Richmond. Nice to meet you, Rafe."

"You too."

"Are you related to Duffy Porter?"

Though it was rude, Mary tuned out his response. She couldn't help it. Rafe made her uncomfortable in a way she hadn't felt in several years. He was tall, good looking, and pleasant enough. He'd even made himself helpful by fetching the ladder for her. Yes, he was certainly charming. Too charming. Men that charming often hid behind winsome, toothy smiles that caught people off guard and made them forget—

"Mary?" Bill looked at her, a slightly amused smile on his lips. "Were you daydreaming?"

He tipped his head toward Rafe, who was also looking at her, only his smile was a tad more expectant.

Rafe chuckled and shook his head. "It's okay." He gestured toward the door. "Maybe we can do lunch another time, when you're not so busy. I'm in town for a couple of weeks."

"I'm sure your uncle is happy about that," Mary said non-committally. She waited until Rafe walked away and then sighed and looked up at Bill. She took his arm and led him away from a cluster of customers to a quiet corner. "Thanks for showing up when you did."

He glanced toward the door. "How did you meet Rafe Porter?"

"He was at the cemetery when I went by there yesterday afternoon to paint."

"Are you reluctant to be with him?"

"Yes. No." She spoke too quickly and perhaps a tad too vehemently. She cleared her throat and looked away. "Something about him rubs me the wrong way," she continued. "Anyway, enough about him."

Briefly, she summed up the events of yesterday and this morning. "I did get a good idea from all of this," she finished. "When I get a chance, I'm going to go through all of Mama's old photo albums to see if I can find a picture of Uncle Paul."

"I'm surprised you don't know more about him," Bill said, scratching his head, "even if he did die young and you never knew him."

"Well, he was always sort of a black sheep," Mary said. "Maybe that's why I feel so drawn to him."

Bill shook his head, his brown eyes suddenly somber. "You're not a black sheep. You're creative and a little quirky, but you're also kind and generous."

A flush crept up his cheeks as he looked away.

Now that was something she'd never heard from Brian's lips, at least not in the latter years of their marriage.

Mary appreciated Bill's words. She knew he was not prone to effusive compliments, so hearing him offer praise truly meant something.

"Thank you," she whispered, suddenly feeling shy and awkward.

He pushed a lock of sandy brown hair from his forehead, *his* smile winsome and not at all too toothy. "No problem."

She grinned back. "So listen, since the shop is busy this morning, what do you say we go ahead and grab a bite to eat real quick at the house? I know it's early, but that will let Martha and Elizabeth eat around noon." She pointed her thumb over her shoulder. "Just give me a second to check with them."

"Sure. I'll wait outside."

The sisters often took turns covering the shop during lunch, so after clearing it with them that she would go first today, Mary collected the teapot she'd purchased from Della and met Bill outside.

They walked in companionable silence up to the house. Mary unlocked the back door and they went into the kitchen. She pulled the teapot from its wrapping and held it aloft in front of the kitchen window. In daylight, it looked even better than it had under the fluorescent lights of the shop. She smiled, pleased with her purchase.

Bill whistled. "Wow, that's really pretty."

"Thanks, I thought so." She pressed it carefully back into its paper cocoon and set it on the counter. "Della found it at a garage sale."

"You mentioned her earlier. She's one of the ladies who sells her stuff on consignment, right?"

Mary opened the refrigerator and got out fixings for sandwiches. "I didn't ask her which garage sale, but I probably should have, so I could ask if they have any other pieces. I'm pretty sure a teapot like this would normally be part of a collection."

After a quick lunch, Bill left to return to work, and Mary hurried to the office to leave the teapot in her desk file drawer. That way it would be handy so she could google the maker's mark. On the way back to the shop, she determined to do all she could to find out what happened with Uncle Paul.

CHAPTER FOUR

Martha watched as Mary returned to work and Elizabeth took her turn at lunch. She was glad that Bill had come to chat a while with Mary. He was a good friend for her, especially after Brian's bitter betrayal. Mary no longer seemed so hesitant since Bill entered the picture. Her confidence had returned, as evidenced by her desire to actually display her work in the store.

She glanced down at the painting, astounded as always by the level of skill Mary possessed.

"That's a nice piece. Is it new?" A woman leaned over the counter for a better look.

Martha turned the painting to give her a better view. "Yes, it's new. My sister painted it."

The woman's eyebrows rose. "Really? She's very talented."

"Thank you." Pride for her sister filled Martha's chest. "I can introduce you to her," she said, looking around. "She just came back from lunch."

The woman waved her hand. "Oh, that's all right. I really need to be going anyway. I just came in because I've been hearing so much about your store."

"Oh? That's wonderful," Martha said. "We've been working really hard to get the store up and going, so it's nice to know people are talking."

The woman sent a sweeping glance around the room. "Well, your hard work shows. It's really lovely. So quaint and inviting."

"Thank you," Martha said. "The barn belonged to our great-grandparents many years ago. They were actually the ones who turned it into a resale shop. We reopened it after our mother passed away."

"We?"

"My sisters and I." Martha pulled a business card out of a vintage card holder next to the cash register. "Mary is the one who did the painting. I'm Martha, and my other sister, Elizabeth, is at the house for lunch."

The woman tapped the card lightly against her palm. "Well, like I said, it's lovely. I'm sure I'll be stopping by again."

"Please do. And tell your friends."

The woman smiled before moving off, and Martha thought what a nice person she was before returning to the cash register to help another customer. Though they stayed busy, Martha's thoughts remained fixed on her parents. She loved her sisters, and telling others about their talents and accomplishments made her so happy. So why hadn't their father ever spoken of *his* brother? They were only two years apart—surely they had been close?

Shortly after noon, the store emptied a bit, and Elizabeth came back from lunch. Martha took a moment to speak to her before she took her turn at the house.

"Elizabeth, do you have a second? I'd like to ask you about something."

"Of course." Elizabeth finished wrapping up a vase, placed it in a bag, and handed it to her customer. She turned to Martha. "What's on your mind?"

"It's Uncle Paul. I haven't been able to get him out of my mind since Mary painted that picture."

"Me neither." She braced one hand on her hip. "I feel like I should remember him more, but it was so long ago."

"I feel the same way."

"Well, we'll find out what we can now. I guess we have Mary to thank for that. What do you think about getting in touch with Aunt Gertrude and the others? I'm sure one of them could tell us something about Uncle Paul. They might even have a few pictures."

Their aunt Gertie was the youngest living sibling and fell between their father and Uncle Paul in the birth order. Other relatives included an uncle who lived in Washington State and three more aunts scattered across Pennsylvania—seven Classen siblings in all.

Martha pushed a stack of receipts across the counter to Elizabeth. "Let's try Aunt Gertrude first. I think she'd probably be the one to ask. I have her number written down in that old phone directory Mama left us. I'll try calling her tomorrow."

Elizabeth laid her hand on Martha's arm. "Okay, but let's let Mary know what we've decided, all right? I wouldn't want her to feel left out. It was her idea, after all."

Martha agreed, thankful for her sweet, sensible elder sister, the peacemaker in the bunch and the one most attuned to the needs of others.

After about an hour the shop emptied out a bit, so Martha went up to the house to look for Aunt Gertie's number. As she thought, she found it in their mother's directory. Struck by a sudden flash of inspiration, Martha flipped back several pages to the *C*s where Uncle Paul's information should be.

She breathed a sigh of disappointment. His name wasn't on the page. Although, now that she thought about it, maybe he'd never lived anywhere else but here. If so, there wouldn't be any reason to have his name in the book.

Well, Aunt Gertrude should be able to tell them what they wanted to know. Unfortunately, being able to tell them and actually telling them were two entirely different things.

Mary hummed quietly to herself as she went about the process of closing up the store. She was tired, and her feet hurt from being on them all day, but her heart was light—probably because at lunch Bill had talked about taking in a movie sometime next week. After years of Brian telling her she was too flighty to have any real friends, it felt wonderful to have someone want to spend time with her.

Elizabeth bumped her in the ribs with her elbow. "What's that smile for?"

Mary glanced at her and then ducked her head and pretended to be engrossed in the stack of dollar bills she was bundling. "Oh, I was just thinking." She shot a quick glance at the clock. "Say, I'm starving. What did Martha say she has planned for dinner?"

"Roast beef and carrots," Martha called as she flipped the CLOSED sign. She paused with her hand on the door lock. "Maybe I'll make some golden potatoes too, if I have enough of them. The roast is already in the oven and should be ready in just under an hour."

"Do you need me to run to the store?" Mary offered, flicking off lights as she walked.

Martha shook her head, but she gave Mary a look that made her think Martha was assessing her.

She eyed her warily. "What?"

"Nothing." Martha shook herself. "Anyway, I'm going to head on up to the house." She looked outside and then back over her shoulder. "Um...would you like to come with me? To help with supper, I mean."

"Me?" Mary peeked at Elizabeth, who looked as dumb-founded as she felt as she jerked her head up from her receipt book and stared.

Mary swallowed her surprise. "Uh, yeah, sure. I'll be right up." When Martha slipped out the door, she turned to Elizabeth. "What do you make of that?"

Elizabeth blinked innocently and stuffed the receipt book into the drawer under the cash register. "What do you mean? Martha asks me to help all the time."

"You, yes. She's never asked me."

"Don't read too much into it," she said, slipping her arm around Mary's shoulders. "I think Martha just wants to make sure you feel included. It's nice."

Nice, yes, Mary thought as she followed Elizabeth up to the house. She loved both of her sisters, but she'd always been closer to Elizabeth, who was a little more understanding of her free-spirited ways. Martha was just so hardworking and pragmatic. Growing up, Mary thought they had very little in common. Maybe that could change now that they were older. Maybe they had more in common than she'd always believed.

And maybe she should try to work a little harder to find out what.

CHAPTER FIVE

O n Tuesday evening, before dinner was ready, Mary made her way to the living room. For as long as she could remember, her mother had kept the family photo albums in the same drawer in the same bureau next to the fireplace. A wealth of memories rushed back as she slid them out, one by one, and stacked them on the floor next to her. The pale pink one lined with lace and frills consisted mostly of pictures of her and her sisters. The blue one was packed with pictures of family vacations.

She pulled out a brown one. This one was older than the others, the leather binding worn and cracked in places. She set it on her lap and then had to push Tink away to keep her from sniffing at the thick pages. This one, Grandma Lois had made. If she was going to stumble across a picture of Uncle Paul, it would be here.

The plastic liners covering the photos crackled as she flipped the pages. Familiar faces peered at her across the years—her grandparents standing in front of the house; her father playing on a wooden rocking horse; Grandma Lois beaming proudly as she pointed to the sign above the barn door. Each picture held a caption written in her grandma's distinctive curlicue writing.

She smiled ruefully to herself as she discovered that what was true for one generation was true for all: parents tended to take fewer and fewer pictures as more children come along. She knew that if she opened the album with her and her sisters' pictures, there would be many of Elizabeth, a few of Martha, and one or two of herself, not counting school portraits. And that's obviously what had happened in her father's family. Paul was the last of seven children, and therefore she would be lucky to find even one picture of him that wasn't a group picture.

Elizabeth poked her head into the living room. She stared at the pile of photo albums and then at the one sitting open on Mary's lap. "Mary? What are you doing?"

At Elizabeth's appearance, Tink had jumped to her feet. Mary took her in her arms and then motioned her sister in. "I'm looking for pictures of Uncle Paul."

Elizabeth knelt on the floor next to her. "Good luck with that. I don't remember any pictures of him in here—at least not any that you could tell what he looked like very well."

Mary handed her the photo album. "Unfortunately, you have a very good memory."

Elizabeth laughed. "This is one time I wish I didn't." She got up and slid open another drawer on the bureau. "Did you check in the rest of the drawers?"

"Not yet."

Mary watched as her sister did so. In the bottom drawer, Elizabeth found another album, this one navy blue. She sat down next to Mary and opened it across their laps. "Let's see what we can find in this."

The first page was labeled "George" at the top. The front and back were covered in chronological pictures of their uncle George, from infancy to elementary school to high school graduation to his wedding photo, where he looked to be in his thirties. Mary remembered someone saying he'd married late in life, relatively speaking, for the times.

The next page was labeled "Mavis," and had the same kind of layout as George's page—baby pictures to her wedding day, where she looked exactly the same as she did in her high school senior portrait.

Four more pages followed, labeled "Bess," "Virginia," "Henry," and "Gertrude," although by the time they got to Virginia, only the front of the page held photos, and most of those that weren't wedding pictures were school portraits. Elizabeth and Mary spent a longer time gazing at each of Henry's pictures—their father had been an extraordinarily cute little boy, and a strikingly handsome man. Mary's eyes filled with tears when she saw her mother's dear face in the wedding picture.

The last page in the album was labeled "Paul." Mary looked at it in astonishment. She hadn't expected to see a baby picture—the last three siblings hadn't had one—but she was surprised to see that the last picture for Paul was his junior year of high school. There wasn't even a senior portrait.

Elizabeth spoke, sounding as bewildered as Mary felt. "Are there pictures missing?"

Mary thought for a moment, then said, "Let me check something." She picked up the brown album and paged through it again, paying particular attention to the group photos at weddings, birthdays, and holiday celebrations. "Look," she said. "Paul appears in these pictures up until a certain age—like on his page, I would guess about seventeen. Any photo taken after that, there's no Paul. It's like he fell off the face of the earth ten years before his death."

"It has to be tied to the reason no one ever talks about him," Elizabeth said. "Whatever that is."

Mary thought a moment and then slid the photo albums to Elizabeth and stood. "Will you put these away? I'm going down to the basement to look through some boxes. I need to find a frame for my painting, but more than that, I'm going to look for clues as to what might have caused the rift between Uncle Paul and the rest of the family. I remember a while ago seeing some boxes marked with his name on them down there."

Elizabeth picked up the photo albums and hugged them tightly to her chest. "Do you want some help? I could..."

She trailed off, and Mary shook her head, sparing her from having to devise an excuse. Elizabeth hated dark, confined spaces and avoided the basement whenever she could. In fact, that was why, after ten years, she had yet to go through the boxes in the basement to see if there was anything they could sell in the shop.

"Don't worry. I'll let you know if I find anything," Mary said, and looked toward the kitchen. "Do we still have those flashlights in the cupboard under the sink?"

Elizabeth pushed one hand to the floor and rose. "I think so, but it's been a while since anyone used them. I have no idea if the batteries are any good."

"No problem. Martha always keeps extras in the pantry."

She went to the kitchen to fetch one of the flashlights. The batteries were still strong, so she headed down into the basement. The old stairs of her parents' home creaked under her feet. Even as a child, she'd hated the rickety old things. There was no back to the steps, and she used to have nightmares of falling through, or worse, being grabbed by the ankle.

"You okay down there?" Elizabeth called from the door.

"I'm fine." Mary shined the light around the damp basement. "Hey, Lizzie, where is the light for this room?"

"Over by the water heater."

Right, if she could remember where the water heater stood. She spotted it hunkered in the corner. Sure enough, a string hung from a bare bulb in the ceiling. Mary crossed to it and pulled. Nothing.

"Where are the spare bulbs?" she called up the stairs.

"On the shelf where Mama used to put her canned goods."

Mary found them and quickly replaced the burned-out bulb with a new one. Light flooded the stone walls and bare cement floor. She rubbed her hands over her arms. It was warm outside, but basements were always cool, and this one was also a little damp.

"Do you see anything?" Elizabeth called. "Do you want me to come down?"

"I haven't started looking yet," Mary said. "I had to replace the bulb. And don't come down those stairs. They're a little tricky."

Elizabeth's light laugh floated down to her. "I know. I used to hate going down those things when we were kids, and I still do. I avoid them as much as possible."

"Tell me about it," Mary muttered. She turned off the flashlight and moved over to the far side of the basement, where plastic tubs and cardboard boxes lined the wall two and three deep from floor to about as high as she could reach. Bracing her hands on her hips, she yelled, "Some things have been moved around since I was down here last. Do you remember where you all put Uncle Paul's things?"

"We marked the ones that were Grandma Lois's after she died, but we stacked them all together," Elizabeth said. "You'll have to look through them to figure out which ones were hers and which ones were Uncle Paul's. Are you sure you don't want me to help?"

Though she was tempted by the offer, Mary did not want to risk Elizabeth slipping and hurting herself on the stairs. "No, I'll do it. You go and see what Aunt Gertie has to say."

Blowing out a breath, Mary set about the task of sorting through boxes and setting the ones marked *Grandma* on the floor. After about twenty minutes, she had a pretty sizable pile. After another twenty minutes, it was pretty obvious that the ones belonging to her grandmother were the plastic tubs. She had peeked in each one, and they were all neatly packed and the contents carefully preserved in paper and bubble wrap. She finally reached the cardboard boxes, which were marked *Uncle Paul*. She made quick work of stacking these to the other side and then came across a large wooden crate that she couldn't move. The top had been nailed on, but, whether from time or neglect to secure it, it wasn't tight enough to keep her from prying it open.

Inside was a painting—pretty but not extraordinary, at least not in her opinion. The frame, however, was exceptional in its beauty and intricate carvings. It was the right size and would make a perfect setting for her painting. Still, she hesitated. If the painting was valuable, why had it been packed away for so many years? But if it wasn't, why had Uncle Paul taken such care storing it?

She squinted in the dim light, trying to make out the painting's distinguishing features. The strokes were confident and steady, not messy or erratic like some contemporary artists she'd seen. Obviously, the person who'd done this work knew what they were doing. Was it worth the risk of damaging it for the sake of removing it from the frame?

"Did you find anything?"

Elizabeth's voice startled her from her thoughts. She set the painting aside and gave the box a shove.

"I think so," she called. "I'll be right up."

As she shifted to pick up the painting again, her foot nudged the flashlight and sent it rolling to a stop against the box the painting had come from. Mary bent to retrieve it. Arrested by some newspapers sticking out from the packing straw, she flicked on the flashlight and shone it into the box.

She plucked the papers from the box and blew away the remaining bits of straw still clinging to the edges. A piece flew into her hair. Another settled onto her nose.

"Great." She removed the offending straw and heaved a sigh. "My hay fever will be going into overdrive."

She uncrinkled the newspaper pages one by one and examined them under the flashlight's yellowish glow. All were classifieds and advertising pages, clearly unwanted enough to be used as packing material. As she unwadded the last one, however, a folded paper fell to the ground. She picked it up and unfolded it. Lines crisscrossed the page. Here and there, rectangles dotted the page. Near the center, a wavy *X* marked the spot.

Which spot? What was it?

Mary frowned as she refolded the paper and slid it into her pocket. Shining the flashlight into the box, she picked through the straw to see what else might lay hidden beneath. Except for a few sheets of newspaper, nothing else remained. She examined each sheet—or almost sheet. The next piece she picked up wasn't even paper, not the notebook kind, anyway.

It was a napkin bearing a bistro logo on the front. She flipped it over. On the back was written, *Target ready. Don't get caught.*

Target?

Mary sighed and stood. She wasn't accomplishing much sitting in a damp basement. Besides, for all she knew, this napkin was nothing more than packing material, just like the newspapers. She shoved the napkin into her pocket to join the map, grabbed the painting, and headed up the stairs.

Glad to be back in a world of warmth and light, she closed the basement door behind her and carried the painting to the kitchen, where Martha had the supper preparations in full swing. She eyed Mary as she laid the painting on the table and stepped back to get a better look.

"What is that?" She tapped the spoon on the edge of the pot she'd been stirring and joined Mary at the table. "You found that in the basement?"

"Uh-huh." She bent over and blew on the painting, dislodging a cloud of dust that quickly had both of them coughing.

"Sorry," Mary said, waving the dust from her face. "It was in a crate marked with Uncle Paul's name. Have you ever seen it before?"

Martha gave one last cough, then handed a wet washcloth to Mary to clean up. "No. It's pretty though, especially that frame."

Mary agreed. The scene was of a lovely country cottage. In the distance, the effects of the setting sun turned fluffy clouds golden. Or was the sun rising? A rough path wound through tall, twisted trees and invited the observer to come in and sit by a cozy fire.

She traced the brushstrokes with her finger. "Why do you suppose Grandma and Grandpa didn't hang it?"

Martha pondered this a moment with her hand resting lightly on her hip. "Maybe it was too painful. If it really was Uncle Paul's, it probably hurt Grandma Lois to look at it after he died, especially if the rift with him was still unresolved."

Mary bit her lip. She hadn't considered that. She nodded. "You're probably right."

Martha shuffled back to the stove and turned the heat on under a pot of green beans.

Mary squinted as she studied the fine nuances of the painting, from the artist's use of color to the intricate brushstrokes. Finally, she straightened with a sigh. "So what do you think, Martha? Should I take it out of the frame? I'd like to use it for my painting. Or should I just leave it as it is and put the entire thing back in the basement?"

Martha sprinkled a bit of pepper into the green beans, then glanced over at the painting. "Well, I'd hate to think of a beautiful piece of art locked away in a musty basement. Won't that ruin it eventually?"

"It was packed in straw, which helped control the dampness, but you're right. If it stays down there too much longer, it probably will get damaged."

Martha tasted one of the green beans, nodded, then put a cover over them and turned to Mary. "I don't think it will hurt to take the frame and leave the painting someplace dry until we decide what to do with it. Or if you feel better, we can ask if anyone in the family wants the painting. If no one says yes, we'll either give it away or get another frame and hang it in the house."

Satisfied with Martha's solution, Mary nodded and moved toward the stove to help with dinner.

"So, tell me about Bill," Martha said. She put on two oven mitts and pulled a ham out of the oven. "I take it things are going well?"

Mary paused with a butter knife hovering over a roll. Martha looked up at her curiously—not with concern or judgment, just a sincere interest that said she wanted insight into her sister's life. Mary willed the muscles in her shoulders to relax and turned her focus to the rolls.

"Yeah, I guess you could say things are going well." She scooped up another glob of butter and spread half of it on a roll. "It's funny being around him again after so many years, but it's comfortable too. Like being with an old friend."

Mary looked up. Sorrow twisted Martha's face as she stared, unseeing, at the steaming pot in front of her. Then she blinked rapidly, grabbed the aluminum foil covering the ham, and peeled back the edges.

"Like you and Chuck?" Mary said gently.

Instead of tears, her words brought a tender smile. "I was very blessed to have Chuck for a husband."

Martha began slicing the ham into thin, even steaks. That was typical Martha. When she was finished with a subject, she simply left off and turned her attention to something else, and there was no sense trying to get her to return to the topic.

Mary proceeded to stack the rolls inside a basket. There were too many for just the three of them, but she knew Martha probably planned to use the leftovers for breakfast. That was one of the many things she admired about her sister—how she could take a basket of leftovers and make them into something extraordinary and tasty. Martha's love language was definitely feeding and caring for her family. While Mary often mistook that for something else, she was beginning to understand the many unspoken things her sister said through her pots and pans.

Warmth spread through Mary's chest, and she crossed to wrap Martha in a hug.

Martha's eyes widened, and she pushed the hair from her forehead with the back of her hand. "What was that for?"

"Just because I don't do it enough," Mary said. She carried the platter of ham to the table just as Elizabeth appeared. She had her phone in her hand, and her face wore a look of consternation.

Martha stepped toward her, drying her hands on her apron. "Is everything all right?"

"To be honest, I'm really not quite sure." Elizabeth set the phone down with a troubled sigh. "That was Aunt Gertrude. I asked her if she could tell me what happened between Uncle Paul and the family all those years ago. She apologized, but she said she *couldn't* tell me, even after I pressed about the pictures from the photo album."

Mary frowned and crossed her arms. "This is all so strange. Did she say why not?"

Elizabeth nodded, and she frowned, her face puzzled. "She did. She said the reason she couldn't say anything was because Daddy forbade it!"

CHAPTER SIX

*D*addy forbade it? But that doesn't make any sense."
Martha stepped forward and picked up the phone,
staring at it as though the phone itself might explain what
was happening. "That doesn't sound anything like the Daddy
we knew."

"Unless..." Elizabeth tugged at the collar of her cotton
dress. "After God, Daddy always put his family first."

Mary looked from Elizabeth to Martha. "Wait, I don't
understand—"

"You mean he would have only done it if he thought he was
protecting his family?" Martha interrupted.

"It's the only explanation I can think of. You?"

Martha hesitated a moment and then nodded. "I agree. It's
the only thing that makes any sense."

"But what could he possibly have been protecting us from?"
Mary leaned forward and pressed her palms to the tabletop.
"What could Uncle Paul have been involved in that would
worry Daddy so much? Drugs? Illegal activities?"

"I don't think it helps to speculate," Martha said, a little too
abruptly, even to her own ears. She shot a contrite glance
toward Mary. "But I understand what you mean. I'm as confused by all of this as you are."

"Beans."

Martha blinked once, then twice. "What? Do you mean you think what I just said was beans?"

Mary laughed and pointed to the stove. "No, I mean your green beans are about to burn."

"Oh!" Martha whirled and snatched the pot off the burner.

"Now, where were we?" Mary paced along the wall behind the table. "What did Daddy feel he had to protect us from—or should I say, who?"

Elizabeth shook her head. "We may never know."

Martha clicked the burner off and set the pot of beans on a pot holder. "I'm not so sure. Just because Aunt Gertrude didn't want to talk, doesn't mean Uncle George or one of the others won't."

Elizabeth nodded. "You're right. Uncle George is the oldest, so he may not feel bound by Daddy's edict, especially since Daddy's no longer with us."

"Exactly." Mary glanced at her watch. "It's six here, so it's only midafternoon in Washington State. Should we call now?"

Martha glanced at the ham cooling on the table, but Elizabeth was already moving toward the phone. Fortunately, though she did not have to look up the number, Uncle George did not answer, so Elizabeth ended up leaving a voice message.

"Well, that settles that, for now anyway." Martha poured the green beans into a bowl and carried them to the table along with the rolls. She'd also made a bowl of potato salad earlier that day, so she removed it from the refrigerator while Elizabeth filled their glasses with tea.

"Let's eat before this all gets cold," Martha said, sliding her chair back. The other two sat down, and Elizabeth said the blessing before they dove into their meal.

Martha pointed to Mary. "Did you tell Elizabeth about the painting you found in the basement with Uncle Paul's things?"

"Oh no, I forgot all about it."

Mary set her fork aside and gave a brief recap. While she spoke, Elizabeth chewed thoughtfully, nodding now and again as she listened.

When Mary finished, Elizabeth set her fork down and smoothed the napkin on her lap. "I agree with Martha. I think it's perfectly fine to use the frame. It's not like it was doing anyone any good down there in the basement anyway. I would like to see the original painting though. By the way you describe it, it sounds lovely."

"I'll show you after supper," Mary said. She turned to Martha. "Did I mention that I also found a map in the box?"

Martha swallowed a bite of bread and shook her head. "What kind of map?"

Mary pushed her chair back and stood. She removed the map from her pocket, pushed the basket of rolls aside, then spread the paper out on the table and smoothed the edges. "At least, I think it's a map."

"It certainly looks like one." Martha leaned closer and squinted, then shook her head. "But what would a map be doing in a box in the basement, and what is it a map of?"

"Good question." Mary pointed to one of the rectangles. "These have to be buildings of some kind, don't you think?"

"Possibly." Martha tapped her temple, thinking. "See how these are all grouped together?" She slid her finger across the paper and pointed. "Like houses."

"If those little squares are houses, then the lines must be streets." Elizabeth traced one of the "streets" and then frowned. "But they're not marked. How would we ever possibly know what it was a map of?"

"It's a crude drawing, for sure." Martha straightened. "Anyway, our dinner is getting cold."

"Right." Mary folded up the map and slid it back into her pocket.

The rest of their meal was completed in a hurry, as Mary was obviously eager to show the painting she'd found to Elizabeth. Martha hid a smile as her sisters hurried to wash up and put away the dishes, then finally ended up shooing them away so she could finish the job herself.

Her hands slowed from scrubbing a pot. How often had their mother done the same thing? Martha and her sisters used to love running wild on the farm, especially in the summer when the days were long. Though they always helped with the supper dishes, more often than not, their mother would send them outside to play before the job was done.

A soft mew sounded near her feet. Martha looked down into Butterscotch's big eyes. As if sensing her sudden melancholy, the cat rubbed his little head across the toe of her shoe.

"Thanks, buddy," Martha said softly. She could always count on him to offer comfort when needed.

Instead of finishing the dishes, Martha left them in the sink to soak, then shut off the kitchen light and went to check on her sisters. This was one time when she wouldn't worry about the work that needed to be done. This time, she'd take a cue from her mother and value the time spent playing instead.

CHAPTER SEVEN

Wednesday morning Mary put the finishing nail into the new frame and then turned the painting toward the kitchen window and the early morning sun to admire her handiwork. Yesterday they'd called the rest of Uncle Paul's sisters, and none had expressed any kind of desire to claim any of his things. In fact, they had refused to speak of him at all, and instead encouraged her to get rid of the things stored in the basement. Since she doubted Uncle George would say anything different than what his siblings had already stated, she had decided to go ahead with the plan to use the frame from Uncle Paul's old painting. Happily, she had managed to remove it with relative ease and with no damage to the painting or the frame. So, her painting now had a beautiful new frame, and the old picture was stored under her bed until she could figure out what to do with it.

She smiled. The frame set off her painting even better than she'd imagined. Its dark grain provided striking contrast to the paler hues, but complemented the long shadow of Uncle Paul perfectly.

At her shoulder, Martha spoke. "It's beautiful."

"It really is," Mary said, not because she meant to boast but because the image of the cemetery stirred something deep inside her heart.

Martha squeezed Mary's hand, and Mary knew she'd understood her intent.

"Do you want to take it back to the barn now?"

Mary glanced at the clock on the wall. "We haven't started breakfast yet."

"We'll have time." Martha released her hand and shrugged. "If not, I'll just toast us up some blueberry bagels."

Mary eyed her sister curiously. This new attitude of Martha's had taken her by surprise at first, but now she rather liked that Martha was doing better at not putting work before everything else. Maybe they were rubbing off on each other. She laid the newly framed painting gently aside.

"It can wait. I need to head outside in a bit to feed the animals anyway."

Now it was Martha's turn to look surprised. Her eyebrows rose, and Mary couldn't hide the twitching of a smile as she carried the coffeepot to the sink to fill with water.

Martha reached for a skillet and set it on the stove, then went to the refrigerator and came back with the eggs. "So what will you work on next? Now that you've finished with this painting, do you have any idea what you would like to do?"

"I haven't really thought about it." Mary measured the coffee grounds into the filter, then snapped the lid closed and started the machine. She leaned against the counter and crossed her arms. "That first painting was very spur of the moment. I'm not even sure I'll do another one, at least not right away. I should probably wait and see if the first one sells."

"Why? It's something you love, and you do beautiful work. Everyone who saw your painting commented on it. I'm sure we'll have no trouble selling anything you create."

"Really?" Mary held her breath. She didn't want Martha to think she was fishing for compliments. Still, her sister's praise was a rare and wonderful thing.

Martha set the eggs down and turned, looking into Mary's eyes. "I'm proud of you, Mary. I know I haven't told you that often enough. I intend to change that going forward."

She turned back to the skillet, as though she hadn't just made the most beautiful and amazing statement. "Now, hand me a spoon."

Mary scrambled to do her bidding. Soon, they had a steaming bowl of eggs and a platter of bacon on the table. Mary poured three cups of coffee and set them next to their plates just as Elizabeth entered the kitchen. Still in her night-gown and robe, she rubbed her eyes and blinked at them sleepily.

"I overslept."

"Yes, you did." Martha pressed one of the cups of coffee into Elizabeth's hands with a playful smile. "Drink this. We've got a busy day ahead."

Elizabeth groaned, but before long she was chatting excit-edly about an idea she'd had for uncovering the mystery behind Uncle Paul's strange separation from the family.

"Grandma Lois's diaries." She set her cup down and waved both hands as she urged her sisters to remember. "When we were kids, she used to read to us from the diary she kept when she was a child. She used to love to write in it. Surely she continued the habit when she got older."

Mary swallowed a sip of coffee. "You think? I don't remember her saying much about her diary after we got older."

"That could have been simply that we got too busy to listen." Martha pushed her empty plate aside and leaned over the table toward Mary. "Did you see anything when you were down there looking through Uncle Paul's things?"

Mary shook her head. "No. I saw plenty of boxes, but I only looked through the ones I thought belonged to him."

"I only hope they didn't get thrown away when she died," Elizabeth said, plucking absently at the edge of her napkin. "There was so much to sort through, we'd be very lucky to still have them."

"True, but it's still worth a shot." Martha gave her hand a pat. "Good thinking, Lizzie. I'll look for them after breakfast."

Mary pushed up from the table and carried her dishes to the sink. "I'll help with the dishes and then head down to feed the animals."

"Let me do the dishes," Elizabeth said, also rising. "You two made breakfast. It's only fair."

Their duties assigned, they each went their separate ways. Mary had just flipped the OPEN sign on the store when Martha appeared, a frown on her lips.

"Uh-oh. I take it that look means you didn't find anything?" Mary let the gingham curtains over the window fall back into place and propped her hands on her hips.

Martha shook her head. "No telling where those books went, but they're not in our basement."

"Do you think one of the other aunts or Uncle George has them?"

"We can check, I suppose, but now that everyone knows we're digging into Uncle Paul's past, they may not be willing to share them."

Mary sighed and went to switch on the cash register. "Well, it was a long shot, anyway." She turned the key, waited for the little blip, then inserted the cash drawer. "Any word from Uncle George?"

Martha carried a basket of fresh baked goods to the display case. "Not yet. I think I'll ask Elizabeth to call him again, just in case he didn't get the message she left."

"Or he could be traveling," Mary said, joining Martha. She watched while Martha arranged a plate of fresh blueberry scones. "Didn't he buy an RV a few years back?"

Martha's hands stilled. "That's true. I forgot about that. I wonder if Elizabeth tried his cell phone?"

Mary was about to suggest she try when the door opened and three familiar figures stepped into the store. Linda, Beverly, and Nancy all carried boxes or bags in their arms—a surefire sign that they'd had a successful shopping excursion. Mary looked over Nancy's shoulder, expecting Della to bring up the rear, and was surprised when Nancy let the door close behind her.

Mary hurried over to them and plucked one of the bags out of Linda's arms. "Did you all go on a special shopping expedition? It's not Monday! Here, let me help you with that."

"Thanks." Linda hefted the remaining bag in her arms and blew a stray lock of brown hair out of her eyes. "You came along just in time. I was losing my grip." She glanced down at the bag. "Though if I keep shopping like this, my husband is likely to say I *have* lost my grip...on reality."

Mary laughed with her and led the way toward the beautiful oak L-shaped counter that Bill had made for them where they could sort through the new things. "Well then, I've got good news for you *and* your husband. The items you gals brought in Monday sold. I've got a check for Della too. Where is she, by the way?"

"Actually, we haven't spoken to her," Beverly said. Though she wasn't all that much older than the others, she had elected to let her hair turn naturally gray. The silver highlights at her temples added sparkle to her blue eyes and always brought images of Mrs. Claus to Mary's mind.

"I tried calling her twice this morning," Beverly continued, "but she never picked up."

"And I tried calling yesterday. The call went straight to voice mail," Nancy added.

"Hmm." Mary set the bag on the table. "That's a little odd. Doesn't she normally go with you on these shopping trips?"

"Usually," Linda said, setting her bag alongside Mary's. "But she does have a sister who lives off somewhere—California, I think. Right, Nancy?"

Nancy nodded. "Yeah. Her name is Charlotte. I think she said she lives in San Diego."

"You think she went to visit her sister? Wouldn't she have let you know that?" Mary asked.

Beverly waved dismissively. "Eh, I'm not worried. Della always has had a mind of her own." She bent and set her box on the floor. "Wait until you see the lace doilies and hand-stitched linens I found. Pristine, I tell you. I bet your Amish customers will love them."

Pushing thoughts of Della aside, Mary folded the flaps back on Beverly's box and stooped to examine her finds. She lifted a white tablecloth with scarlet embroidery along the hem.

"Ooh, this is really beautiful."

Reaching into her pocket, she took out a pen and began labeling stickers for each item. The corresponding numbers were recorded in a small notepad so an accurate tally could be kept each week and payment delivered to the consignees. It was a dated system, but it worked—at least until Mary could talk her sisters into investing in an up-to-date computer program. Right now, it was Elizabeth who was digging in her heels and insisting they had no need of new software. Other times, it was Martha. Either way, Mary was stuck with pen and paper, so she jotted the numbers in her notebook and then flipped the cover closed.

"All right, I think that's all of it." She stood, crossed to the cash register, removed three envelopes, and handed them out to Nancy, Linda, and Beverly.

She pressed her hands to her hips. "What about Della? Do you think she'll be by later this week so I can pay her, or should I try stopping by her apartment?"

Nancy tucked her envelope into a pocket of her purse. "I wouldn't worry about it. I'm sure she'll be in touch. In fact, we'll have her call you if we hear from her first."

"That would be great. Thank you, ladies," Mary said.

She gave them a wave and a smile as they turned to go, but deep down she felt a small niggle of concern for Della. She didn't like it that the older woman hadn't been in touch, especially since she'd said they would hear from her yesterday. Then again, maybe she didn't know anything more about the cups, so just didn't call. It had to be the motherly instinct inside her going into overdrive that had her nervously pacing. Still, she couldn't quell the tiny spark of concern that said something wasn't right—and that she needed to check on Della.

Soon.

CHAPTER EIGHT

Mary checked the number for Della in her contact list and called again. She paced along the porch, swatting absentmindedly at a fly. As before, the phone rang several times before going to voice mail.

Stifling a frustrated sigh, she left a brief message and hung up. Including the one she'd just left, Mary had left four messages—one yesterday and three today—and Della had yet to return her call. What could she possibly be doing? Where could she have gone, and why wasn't she checking her messages?

"Still nothing?"

Elizabeth pushed open the screen door and stepped onto the porch with Mary. Her face was slightly flushed from having been elbow deep in sudsy water, but she had insisted that she be the one to help clean up the supper dishes so Mary could try Della one more time.

Mary shook her head and slipped her phone into the pocket of her jeans. "I just don't understand it. Della told me she'd call me." She stopped pacing and turned to look Elizabeth in the face. "I really would like to drive over to her apartment to check on her. Would you mind going with me?"

Instead of accusing her of overreacting as Martha might have, Elizabeth reached behind her back and untied her apron strings. "Of course. But give me a minute to freshen up before we go."

Mary's heart warmed for her strong, supportive sister. Thanks to her temperament, Elizabeth was naturally the peacemaker, but her kindness and generosity of spirit were things she had carefully cultivated during her quiet times with the Lord. Mary had learned a lot from her growing up. Now that they were adults, she knew she had much more to learn.

Martha walked up the path from the barn with Pal following close behind. Her hair was tucked up into a bun on her neck, but a few wisps blew into her eyes. She pushed them behind her ears as she climbed the porch steps. "Did I hear you girls say you're going somewhere?"

"We're going to check on Della," Elizabeth said before Mary could respond. She laid her apron across the porch rail, a determined glint in her eye. "Della told Mary she'd call her and hasn't, and Mary has been trying to call her for two days. She's worried."

"Actually, Linda, Nancy, and Beverly have been trying longer than that," Mary said, sounding defensive but feeling like the information might add credibility. To her surprise, Martha didn't question her concern. Instead, she reached for the doorknob.

"Do you mind if I go with you? I'd like to know she's okay myself."

Mary frowned and crossed her arms. "You're worried too?"

"She lives alone. It wouldn't hurt to check on her," Martha said, neither affirming nor denying any worry on her part. "Besides, I'm running low on flour. After we check on Della, we can swing by the grocery store and pick some up, if that's all right with you."

"Deal." Mary crossed to the screen door and held it open while her sisters passed through. "I'm going to grab my purse. I'll meet you both back down here in a few minutes."

Upstairs, Mary scrambled to find her purse and cram her feet into a comfortable pair of shoes. She met Elizabeth on the stairs. She, too, had changed. Instead of a blue shirt and jeans, she now wore a pretty floral blouse and denim skirt. It wasn't the plain clothes she used to wear when Mary first moved back to Bird-in-Hand, but it was still very conservative and simple. It was a very becoming look, one that suited Elizabeth's modest taste.

Soon, Martha joined them. It didn't take long for the three of them to pile into Mary's car and drive the short distance across town to Della's apartment. Bird-in-Hand was not large, and was limited on conveniences, but when they couldn't find something here, New Holland and Lancaster were both just a short drive away.

In minutes, they had parked and were heading up the curved brick path that led to the main door of the apartment complex. Though the building was quite old, it still retained some of its quaint charm. It was painted a cheery yellow, and flower boxes lined all of the first- and second-story windows. Elizabeth pointed toward the rows of doorbells, each marked with an apartment number.

"Do we know which one is hers?"

"24B," Mary said. When her sisters looked at her with their eyebrows raised, she shrugged. "Nancy told me."

Easing past her sisters, Mary marched up to the door and pushed the buzzer to Della's apartment. No one answered. She waited a moment and then pushed the buzzer a second time.

"Maybe she's not home," Elizabeth whispered.

"Why are you whispering?" Martha asked, also whispering.

The door swung open, and all three sisters jumped back. A young woman pushing a stroller eased the door wide, caught sight of Mary, Elizabeth, and Martha, then stopped and propped the door open with one hand.

"Oh, sorry. I didn't see you there," she said, wiggling the stroller back inside.

"Here, let me get the door for you." Mary moved to the other side, then grabbed the handle and pulled it wider while the woman angled the stroller through.

"Thanks." She smiled gratefully and wiped the sweat from her forehead with the back of her hand. "My husband and I never realized how much stuff we would have to lug around when we had a baby."

The sisters laughed and watched as the young woman expertly navigated the rest of the way out to the parking lot. When she rounded the corner, Mary dropped her gaze to peer at the door handle still clutched in her hand…and at the door it was attached to, standing wide open. Slowly, she lifted her eyes to meet her sisters' and then swept her free hand with a flourish to usher them inside.

"24B?"

Elizabeth stepped forward. "Yep."

"Wait." Martha put out her hand and snagged Elizabeth by the sleeve. "She didn't buzz us in. What if someone sees us? What will we say? What if they think we're up to no good?"

Elizabeth pulled at the sides of her skirt. "Even if someone does see us, do you seriously think they'll worry that we're here to rob the place?"

Martha frowned and peeked into the empty apartment lobby. "Probably not. All right then, let's go."

Elizabeth led the way, one finger raised as she read the numbers aloud on each green door, but when they arrived at Della's apartment, she stepped aside to let Mary knock. Oddly, after only one knock, the door creaked open. All three sisters stared at it in amazement.

Finally, Martha broke the silence. "Is she home?"

"I don't know." Mary jabbed the door open a little wider with her thumb. "Della?"

At the silence that followed, she poked her head into the apartment. "Della, are you home? It's Mary Baxter from Secondhand Blessings."

A chill traveled Mary's spine—a sense of foreboding, perhaps, that something wasn't right—but she straightened and stepped through the door the rest of the way.

"Are you going in?" Elizabeth said, her voice a loud stage whisper.

"What choice do we have?" Mary whispered back.

The door to Della's apartment opened onto a narrow hall. Family pictures lined the wall, including one of a shaggy, long-haired dog.

Mary froze. Did Della have pets? If so, was one of them about to come tearing down the hall in a frenzy of biting teeth?

She listened for the scrabbling of paws on the laminate floor or the warning bark of a protective sheepdog. Hearing nothing, she turned and beckoned for Martha and Elizabeth. There was no telling what they would find once they got inside the apartment, but one thing was certain...

Mary did not want to face it alone.

CHAPTER NINE

Della's apartment was small and messy. Very messy. Martha stepped over a couch cushion and two broken picture frames before she realized this wasn't an everyday, ordinary mess. Della's apartment had been ransacked.

"Oh, crumbs," she whispered, her eyes widening in amazement.

Elizabeth and Mary came to the realization in the same moment as she did. Mary darted toward the bedroom calling Della's name. Behind her, Elizabeth called, "Don't touch anything!"

Martha crossed to stand next to her. "Go and check the kitchen," she said, in as calm a voice as she could muster. "I'll look in the bathroom and the laundry."

Elizabeth whirled and made a beeline for the kitchen. Martha was tempted to relay the same advice she'd given Mary and tell her not to touch anything, but Elizabeth had gone before she could form the words.

Swallowing hard, Martha went down the hall to the bathroom. Here, too, things lay strewn across the floor. Embroidered hand towels lay in a heap, the medicine cabinet door hung open, the contents of various vitamin and aspirin bottles littered the floor, and the shower curtain had been half-pulled from its rings.

Martha bit the inside of her cheek, thinking. What could an intruder have possibly been looking for in a bathroom?

She stuck her head into the hall. "Anything?"

"Nothing here," Mary said, emerging from the bedroom, "but it's a mess inside."

"Here too," Martha said.

"Nothing in the kitchen," Elizabeth said, sounding relieved. "Except that I don't think there's a single unbroken plate left in there. Even the trash can was emptied onto the floor."

After a moment, Mary took a quivering breath. "Is there anywhere else we can look?"

Martha pointed to a white louvered door midway down the main hall. "What's that?"

It was a laundry closet. With the washer, dryer, and a small water heater packed inside, there wasn't much room for anything else.

A small bit of the tension seeped from Martha's shoulders. "She's not here. The place is empty."

"Her phone is working," Elizabeth said from behind them.

Martha and Mary turned to look. Elizabeth stood next to the telephone, which oddly had not been disturbed. A small answering machine sat next to it with the number twelve blinking in bright red on the screen.

"Does that mean she has twelve new messages?" Martha said.

Elizabeth nodded. "Unfortunately, there's no way to tell how old these messages are without touching something." She glanced at Mary. "Is there?"

Mary shook her head and pulled her phone from her pocket. "No. I don't think we have any choice. We need to call the police."

Though she sounded certain, she waited until Martha nodded at her. While she spoke to the police, Martha drew Elizabeth aside.

"What do you think?" She whispered so as not to disturb Mary, whom she could hear relaying the address to Della's apartment.

"I don't know what to think," Elizabeth said. "What do we really know about Della? Does she have any family? Friends? Who could we talk to that would have any idea what happened here?"

"Friends, we know," Martha said. "Beverly, Nancy, and Linda."

"But they said they hadn't talked to her in almost a week."

"True." Martha frowned. She glanced at the answering machine with its glowing indicator light. "Sure wish we could listen to those messages."

"Four of them we know are from Mary," Elizabeth said.

"That still leaves eight." Martha's gaze drifted to the stack of books sitting next to the phone and the one lying open on top. It was an address book. She stretched her hand toward it.

Elizabeth gasped and grabbed her arm in warning. "Martha, what are you doing? You said not to touch anything."

"I'm not going to touch it," Martha replied evenly, though her knees were shaking and her arms felt like lead. She let her gaze run down the page. "What is Della's sister's name?"

"The police are on their way." Catching sight of them, Mary rushed back into the room and stared openmouthed at Martha. "What on earth are you doing? Martha, this is a crime scene."

"I told her the same thing," Elizabeth said, crossing her arms.

"I'm still not touching anything," Martha said. "I'm just looking. Mary, what is Della's sister's name?"

Mary looked at her, frowning. "Charlotte," she said.

She dropped her gaze back to the page. "Bingo! Charlotte. That's got to be her sister."

Elizabeth looked down at the page and then at her. "Are you sure?"

Martha looked at Mary again. "Where does Charlotte live?"

Mary thought a moment before answering. "California somewhere...oh—San Diego."

"Then I'm positive." Martha pointed to the book. "Charlotte Matlin from San Diego. Right there. See?"

Elizabeth and Mary leaned in to see. Martha reached into her purse and took out a pen. "I'll write it down."

"Don't bother." Mary tapped several keys on her phone. "There, I added her to my contacts."

"Good." There were definitely some benefits to technology.

After a few minutes, Martha paced to the window and looked out onto the parking lot. "Goodness, it sure seems like it's taking the police a long time to arrive."

Mary glanced at her watch. "Not really. It's only been five minutes."

"Five minutes!" Martha sighed nervously and moved away from the window. "Well, I can't just stand here doing nothing."

"Me neither," Mary agreed quickly. "I say we look around and try to see if we can tell what happened."

"As long as we're careful not to disturb anything," Martha warned.

The three looked at one another for a moment.

"All right, so let's try to figure out how they got in." Elizabeth moved toward the window. "Do any of the locks look tampered with?"

Mary crossed to the door and bent to examine the latch. "This one looks fine."

"What about scratches on the lock? Someone may have tried to pick it," Martha said.

Mary shook her head and straightened. "It looks clean. Just normal wear."

"The window looks good too, though we are on the second floor. A person would need to have a ladder or something to climb through a window." Elizabeth dropped the curtain. "Should we even bother to check the bedrooms?"

Martha nodded. "It's worth it to be thorough. I'll take the guest room."

Elizabeth pointed. "I'll check the master."

Mary went the opposite way. "I'll look at the veranda."

Della's apartment was laid out pretty simply. The outside door opened onto the open-plan living room and kitchen. Off of the kitchen was a door leading to a small veranda and another door to the guest bathroom. The master bedroom and guest bedroom were on opposite sides of a narrow hall.

Except for the mess, the bedrooms looked normal. Martha met Elizabeth back in the hall and turned for the veranda.

"Anything?" she asked when Mary came back inside.

Mary nodded, and excitement shone in her eyes. "Maybe. Della's plants were knocked over, as if someone upset them when they climbed over the rail."

Elizabeth frowned doubtfully. "I don't know. It's been pretty windy. Could it have been the wind that knocked them over?"

"Maybe. Let's check the door," Martha said. She was disappointed when the lock appeared to be completely free of any incriminating scratches. She threw up her hands in exasperation. "I don't understand. How did the intruder get in if they didn't have to pick one of the locks?"

Elizabeth inhaled sharply. "You don't think it was someone Della knew, do you?"

The implications made Martha's heart pound. Someone had come into Della's apartment and torn it apart, and now she was missing.

"Hold on...what is that?" Mary brushed past them and bent to pick up something from the floor just outside the veranda door.

"What is it, Mary?" Elizabeth asked.

Martha hastened over to examine the object in Mary's palm. It was small—half the size of a dime—and triangular shaped. One side was shiny and silver, the other plain white.

Martha frowned. "That almost looks like—"

Mary grasped it by the corner and brought it up to her eyes. "It's a piece of a credit card. That must be how they got in."

Elizabeth scratched her head. "I don't understand. How would a credit card help?"

Mary made a sliding motion. "A credit card is slim and flexible enough to slide into the crack between the door and the jamb. But it's also sturdy enough to push back the lever and slip the door open, even if it's locked. Of course, it wouldn't work on a deadbolt, but if Della didn't bolt the door..."

Martha stared at her in amazement. "How on earth do you know all of that?"

Mary's face reddened. "One of the many random things Brian taught me."

Brian again. Martha shook her head. "Well, this is certainly something we will need to show the police. What this means is that Della didn't let the person in, so it's probably not someone she knew well."

As if on cue, a knock sounded on the front door, followed by the entrance of two uniformed police officers.

"I'll go speak with them," Mary said, hurrying over to the officers.

When she'd gone, Elizabeth turned wide eyes to Martha. "This looks bad, doesn't it? Something terrible has happened to Della."

"It doesn't look good," Martha agreed, "but we shouldn't jump to conclusions about Della. It's possible she wasn't even here when her apartment was broken into."

Elizabeth thought a moment, and then a small bit of the concern cleared from her face. "You're right. Wondering if she was will only make us worry."

Martha agreed, but deep down, she was just as worried as Elizabeth. Her instincts warned her that something terrible had happened to Della. Worse, she had a strange feeling that finding out exactly what that something was would require all of their attention and skill.

CHAPTER TEN

Mary rubbed her hand wearily over her face. Speaking with the police officers had taken much longer than she had expected. At one point, she'd even felt a little nervous as the officers' questions became more pointed—what was her connection to Della? How long had they known each other? Did Della have any enemies? With not much information to give, she'd found herself repeating "I really don't know" more times than she cared to admit.

Elizabeth leaned forward from the back seat. "Are you all right, Mary? Would you like me to drive for you?"

Mary shook her head. "I'm fine, Elizabeth. Just tired and more than a little worried."

"We're all worried," Martha said. She tugged the seat belt away from her neck and sighed. "I just wish we had some idea of when this happened and whether or not Della was even home."

Mary tapped the steering wheel with her finger. "We need to call her sister. Even if Della didn't go to visit her, she may have some idea of where she could have gone."

"Assuming Della wasn't home when the break-in occurred," Martha said.

"Exactly." Mary motioned toward the shoulder of the road. "We could call her now. Should I pull over?"

"Mary, wait." Elizabeth laid her hand on Mary's shoulder. "Let's think about this a moment. If Della didn't go to visit her sister, calling her with news that she might be missing seems a bit irresponsible, especially since we have no idea what happened."

Mary bit her lip, considering what her own reaction would be if a stranger called with news that one of her sisters was missing. She nodded and pressed her foot to the accelerator. "You're right. I didn't think about that."

Martha sighed. "There must be some way of finding out. Besides Beverly, Nancy, and Linda, who are Della's friends? If we knew that, we might be able to ask around without causing too much worry."

"We could find out where she went to church," Elizabeth suggested, tapping the back of the seat. "And work. Does she have a job?"

Mary shook her head. "That one I know the answer to, and it's no. Della retired several years ago from the bank downtown."

"But that does give us a lead," Martha said. "Surely she had friends at the bank. We could ask there if any of them keep in touch. Maybe we'll get lucky and stumble onto a clue as to what happened, or where she's gone."

"Good idea, Martha." Mary hit the turn signal and pulled into their driveway. Talking things through with her sisters already made her feel a little better. At least she wasn't trying to figure this out alone.

She parked the car, and the three of them went inside. Mary set her purse down and held out her hands to her sisters.

"Before you two settle in for the night, would you mind if we prayed for Della? I'm still hoping she simply went out of town to visit family, but I don't think it would hurt to say a prayer for her safety, regardless."

"Of course, Mary." Elizabeth set her purse and sweater down and grasped her sister's hand.

Martha agreed they needed to seek the Lord on Della's behalf, and the three formed a tight circle. Mary voiced the prayer, her sisters' murmurs of encouragement and agreement giving her confidence. She even surprised herself with her fervor. Usually it was Martha who led in such things, or even Elizabeth, though she had a much quieter way about her. This time, she was the one leading, and it felt good to finally be finding her own faith instead of relying on her sisters'.

When she said amen, both Martha and Elizabeth gave her hands a squeeze before letting go. "Thank you, Mary," Elizabeth whispered.

Mary nodded. "Should I make us some tea?"

Elizabeth glanced at the clock and then declined with a shake of her head. "I know it's early, but I'm exhausted. I think I'll take a warm bath and head to bed."

"Me too," Martha said, rubbing her eyes wearily. "I think all this business with Della has worn me out." She cast an apologetic glance at Mary. "Sorry."

"It's all right," Mary said. "I won't be far behind you."

She bade her sisters good night, but instead of following them upstairs, she turned for the kitchen. Tink was asleep on the mat near the door but raised her head the moment Mary entered. Her tail wagging, she scurried over to greet her with happy, bouncing pats on Mary's legs.

Mary laughed and gave Tink's ears a tickle. Inside her pocket, her phone vibrated, and she realized she hadn't checked her messages all afternoon. A text from Bill caught her eye.

EVERYTHING OKAY?

She scrolled up to see why he was asking. Apparently, she'd missed several texts from him. His concern was probably caused by the fact that she hadn't responded to any of them.

She pulled out a chair at the table, lifted Tink onto her lap, and typed out a reply.

I'M FINE. BEEN GONE ALL AFTERNOON, BUT HOME NOW.

Her phone pinged a moment later.

WORK?

Giving the dachshund one last pat, Mary lowered her to the floor and then crossed the kitchen and laid the phone on the counter. How to respond to that? She wouldn't lie to him. She picked up the phone.

SORT OF. ONE OF THE LADIES WHO SELLS HER STUFF ON CON-SIGNMENT AT THE STORE HAD HER APARTMENT BROKEN INTO.

Instead of hitting SEND, Mary reread her message, then deleted it and dialed Bill's number. He answered on the first ring.

"Hey."

At the sound of his warm voice, Mary instantly felt like smiling. "Hi. Sorry I didn't answer you sooner."

"No problem. Is everything okay?"

"Not exactly," she said with a sigh.

While she explained where she'd been, she filled Tink's water bowl and then put a kettle of water on the stove to heat. Bill listened quietly, something she deeply appreciated. In no time at all, he'd become someone she looked forward to telling things to, but not necessarily because she needed his input.

"I completely understand why you're worried," he said when she finished. "I'll be praying for her too."

"Thank you, Bill." She poured hot water over the tea bag in her cup then carried it with her to the table. "Hopefully, the police will be able to tell us something soon."

"Did they say they would be in touch?"

She wrapped the tea bag string around her finger and dipped the tea bag gently into the hot water. "No, but if we haven't heard something by tomorrow afternoon, I may call to see if there's any new information."

"Mmm." There was a brief pause, and then Bill said, "What about your uncle? Were you able to learn anything new about him today?"

Mary wrung the tea bag against her spoon and then discarded it on an empty saucer. "Goodness, I haven't even thought about Uncle Paul. We were so wrapped up in checking on Della, I forgot to ask Martha if she heard from our uncle George in Washington."

Making a mental note to ask Martha in the morning, Mary filled Bill in on their plans to speak with the other members of the family about Grandma Lois's diaries in case any of them made mention of Uncle Paul.

"It certainly is strange," he said when she finished. "I wish I could help."

"I know," Mary said. "Thanks for offering." She fingered the handle on her cup, realizing as she did that she was enjoying talking to Bill and didn't want it to end. "So tell me about your day. How were things at work? Were you able to finish up at the Wilson place?"

Along with installing windows and doors, Bill was customizing under-the-eaves storage for an upstairs bedroom in the Wilsons' old farmhouse.

"It's all done. As for the rest of my day..." He laughed. "It wasn't nearly as exciting as yours. The most interesting thing that happened was a woman called about a bid for a new job. Her husband is sick, and she needs to make a few modifications to her house."

"Anybody I know?"

"I don't think so. I'm going by there tomorrow afternoon for measurements. Oh, and I bumped into that Porter guy at the gas station downtown."

Mary's throat went suddenly dry. She set her cup down with a thump. "Rafe? I mean, Duffy Porter's nephew?"

Bill continued, oblivious to her discomfort. "Uh-huh, that's him. I thought he was just in town visiting."

"He is...at least, that's what he told me. Why?"

"He was buying paint, quite a bit of it, actually. I just thought it was weird for somebody who was only going to be around a few days."

Paint? Mary frowned. "Did he say what he was doing with it?"

"No...well...to be honest, I really didn't ask. I only mentioned it because you acted a little uncomfortable the last time

I saw you with him. I figured you might want to know it seems he's going to stick around a little longer."

"Oh. Thanks, Bill." Mary shook the disturbing feelings sparked with the mention of Rafe Porter from her head. "Well, anyway, I'm glad we talked tonight. I'll let you know what I find out about Della tomorrow."

"Okay. Good night, Mary," Bill said, his voice a warm, masculine rumble in her ear.

"Good night." She waited a moment and then disconnected. Here was something different. With Brian, he'd always been the one to hang up first, oftentimes even before she'd said goodbye. Bill always lingered, always gave her the impression that he was reluctant to let her go.

The smile born of that realization was cut abruptly short as images of Rafe Porter's face flashed into her mind.

Bending low, she scooped up Tink and carried her to the stairs, switching off lights as she passed. Strangely, she found herself hoping that Bill was wrong about Rafe—and that he hadn't changed his mind about staying in Bird-in-Hand. She couldn't deny that having him in town made Bird-in-Hand feel small, like the space was too tight for the two of them, and it troubled her.

And that, of course, was the problem.

It shouldn't trouble her. She shouldn't feel anything at all about whether he stayed or went.

She entered her bedroom and closed the door tight, sensing as she did so that she was trying futilely to close something else out altogether.

CHAPTER ELEVEN

Reddy's strident warble roused Mary early the next morning. She pried her eyelids open with a groan and rolled onto her side. Normally, she didn't mind being awakened by rooster alarm, but after a night worrying about Della, she resented being yanked from her fitful four hours of sleep. She'd tossed and turned, then finally logged on to her computer. She'd been surprised to discover how active Della was on social media. She found accounts for her on both Facebook and Instagram.

"Thanks a lot, Reddy," she mumbled, and tugged the covers over her head. No good. He seemed to call all the louder, his voice winding up like an air raid siren. At one point, he even seemed to hit another octave altogether.

Throwing off the blankets, Mary sat up, swung her legs over the edge of the bed, and stomped to the window. "All right, all right, enough! I'm up, Reddy."

Just like that, he quit—like hitting the snooze on an alarm clock. How was it possible the old bird knew the exact moment her feet hit the floor?

Mary shook her head and stumbled to the bathroom to wash up. Today would be a long day. She still needed to inventory all the new consignment items, plus clean and straighten the shelves she had been promising Elizabeth she would do since last week. Midway through brushing her teeth, her phone chimed, reminding her that she'd set it to inform her of any notifications, like email or Facebook messages—

She spit into the sink and, wiping a towel over her mouth, hurried to the nightstand in her room to collect her phone. Maybe there was a way to see if Della had gone out of town without involving her sister. Maybe Della was posting pictures from some sunny, exotic location, making all of Mary's worries silly and futile.

She plopped onto the bed, logged in to Facebook with two quick taps, and searched for Della's name. She found it easily and clicked on her page. Just like last night, the most recent post was unchanged. It was from a couple of days ago and was just a picture of a new restaurant she hoped to try out. Mary sighed. She'd been hoping for something more recent. Still…

She kept scrolling, further than she had last night, past a couple of recipe videos, a shared meme spouting encouragement during difficult circumstances, and stopped on a photo of a teapot. Her teapot. The one she'd purchased from Della on Monday. The description with the photo was simply Della talking about her garage sale "finds" and her plans to sell them on consignment. Over fifty people had liked the photo, several more left comments asking for information to purchase. Thankfully, Della told them exactly how to get to Secondhand Blessings. She even included the address.

Free promotion, Mary thought with a smile. She scrolled further. Apparently, Della was in the habit of posting pictures of the items she purchased. Along with an array of dishes and pottery, pictures of vintage jewelry, lamps, and even some furniture dotted her time line.

"Hmm." Mary tapped her lip with her finger. Della had listed the teapot on her page. A couple of days later, her apartment was ransacked, and Della disappeared. Could her disappearance be somehow connected to the teapot? Could the person who broke into Della's apartment have been looking for it, hoping to get it before she took it to Secondhand Blessings? Certainly, she posted plenty of pictures, but if it was something else the intruder was after, wouldn't her apartment have been targeted sooner?

Mary weighed her options. It was entirely possible she was off track, but she figured it was better to give this information to the police and be wrong than to withhold something that could lead them to Della's whereabouts.

Her mind made up, she set her phone down and crossed to the closet to change out of her pajamas. First thing this morning, she'd go to the police station, show them Della's Facebook page, and tell them about the teapot. After that, she'd stop at the bank where Della had worked, just to see if any of them still kept in touch and could tell her where Della might possibly have gone. Of course, that meant she would need to ask Martha to fill in for her at the store. She hurried downstairs to look for her.

"Goodness, you're up early. This is getting to be routine," Martha greeted as Mary entered the kitchen. "Do you want some coffee?"

"No, thanks. I have a favor to ask." Briefly, she explained what she'd discovered and what she intended to do.

Martha wiped her hands on her apron as she listened. "Of course I can fill in for you."

Mary bit her lip. "You don't think I'm encouraging the police to chase a rabbit trail, do you?"

"I think it's best not to keep anything from them that might be of use," Martha said, pushing her toward the door. "Now, go, and don't worry about the store. Elizabeth and I will manage until you get back."

Mary turned for the hall and the spacious office that opened off the end. For years, her parents had operated their business out of the kitchen, with her mother tackling the inventory at the table and her father managing sales receipts and overhead. It had seemed only right that the sisters do the same. But the recent addition of a computer, copier, and fax machine had been deemed impractical for the counter next to the coffeepot—hence the new office.

A cumbersome wooden desk dominated one corner, which Martha and Elizabeth happily shared. Mary occupied a small, ornate writing desk she had purchased at a flea market. It was situated near the window, which offered her an expansive view of the barn and the rolling hills beyond.

Mary hurried to her desk and opened the bottom file drawer and pulled out the teapot. She unwrapped it and took a picture of it with her phone, then stowed it back in the drawer.

Putting her phone back in her pocket, she turned toward the front door to collect her keys and handbag. Outside, her shoes crunched loudly on the gravel drive. The clock on her car dash said seven thirty, but by the time she got to the East Lampeter Township police department, it would be closer to eight. She only hoped whoever she spoke to there didn't laugh her out of the station.

She started the engine, put the car in REVERSE, and was preparing to back out of the driveway when a flurry of movement from the direction of the shop caught her eye. The door flew open, and Martha came barreling out, waving her arms high above her head. On her heels, Elizabeth looked almost as panicked.

Mary's heart thumped inside her chest. What was going on? She rolled down the window and leaned out.

"Martha?"

"Stop!" Martha yelled. "Mary, you can't leave."

Mary tightened her grip on the steering wheel. "Why not? What's wrong?"

Elizabeth huffed to a stop next to Martha at the car and rested her elbow against the door while she caught her breath.

"It's the store, Mary," she panted. She pressed her hands to her cheeks, her eyes wide and disbelieving. "Someone broke into the store! Again!"

CHAPTER TWELVE

Mary blinked, trying hard to process what Elizabeth had said, but failing miserably. "What do you mean—?"

The car jerked, and Mary realized she still had it in REVERSE. She jammed it into PARK and then drew a breath to steady herself. "What do you mean, someone broke into the store? Like last time?" Just last month a woman had broken a window to gain access to the shop.

Martha shook her head. "No, not like last time. The door is pushed open." Martha's face was red, and sweat dotted her lip. She wiped it away and then fluttered her hands toward the barn. "I thought for a moment that we had forgotten to lock it, but then I saw the stuff on the floor—"

"You went in?" Mary interrupted.

Elizabeth pushed her hair out of her eyes. "We went in like always. As soon as we realized something had happened, we came straight back to the house to call the police."

Mary's breathing slowed. "Good. Okay."

Think!

Why did her brain feel like it was in a fog? She inhaled deeply, then shut off the car. "All right, let's call the police."

She climbed from the car and shut the door with a bang. Seeing Martha startle, Mary crossed to her and clasped her arm. "Are you all right?"

Martha licked her lips. "It was just such a shock, that's all. I can hardly believe it."

"Of course you can't," Elizabeth said. "None of us can. Two times in two months?" She looked at Mary, her chin trembling. "We don't keep anything of great value. Everything we sell is used. Do you think they were looking for cash?"

Mary shook her head, as helpless to understand what had happened as her sisters. "I have no idea, but we'd better get the police over here to have a look around."

She ushered her sisters back into the house. In the entryway, she pulled her phone from her pocket.

Mary placed the call and then handed the phone to Elizabeth. "Maybe you should talk to him." Elizabeth was the one Officer John Marks had relied on for information about the first break-in.

Elizabeth agreed. Her voice quavered at first but grew stronger as she told John why she was calling. After a moment, she hung up and handed the phone back.

"He said he's on his way. It should only be a few minutes."

Martha gave a curt nod. Her vim obviously returning, she braced her hands on her hips and stuck out her chin. "Did he say what we should do until he gets here?"

"He said just to stay in the house." Elizabeth motioned toward the hill. "He told us not to go near the barn until he has a chance to look things over."

Elizabeth straightened her collar. She was not a vain person, but Mary had noticed that she seemed more aware of her appearance since John entered the picture.

Mary claimed Elizabeth's hand and gave it a pat. "Tell me what you and Martha saw down at the barn. Did the door look damaged?"

"The jamb was splintered," Elizabeth said. "Martha thinks whoever broke in may have kicked the door in."

Mary frowned. "How did we not hear that? Surely Pal would have warned us if something was going on. Tink is pretty good about sounding the alarm too."

Elizabeth's face paled. "The animals. Do you think they're all right?"

The three fell silent.

"I can walk around and check," Mary said.

Elizabeth's gaze jumped from Mary to Martha. "John said to wait inside the house."

No one spoke for a moment, and then Martha nodded. "Elizabeth is right. We should stay put until the police get here."

Though Mary didn't like it, she knew her sisters were right. She paced and counted the minutes until the rev of an engine drew the three of them to the door.

Elizabeth peeked out the window and then let out a sigh of relief. "It's John."

Throwing open the door, she scurried outside to meet him. Mary and Martha followed more slowly and then stood listening while Elizabeth filled him in on what they had found.

John nodded and motioned them toward the house. "All right, why don't you wait inside while I go and take a look? I've got more officers coming. We'll survey the scene, and once it's clear, I'll bring you ladies in to see what, if anything, is missing."

Martha and Elizabeth nodded and moved quickly inside, but Mary stood watching as John walked the short distance to the barn. He slowed as he neared the door, and his hand moved defensively to his hip. She couldn't watch any longer. Whirling, she hurried up the steps and joined her sisters in the house.

To all of their relief, John returned just a short time later with good news to report. Though he confirmed the store had indeed been broken into, there did not appear to be extensive damage. He also reassured them that the animals were fine, drawing a huge sigh of thanksgiving from all three.

"If you all are ready," John continued, "I'd like for you to come down and see if you can spot anything missing."

Outside the shop door, Mary slowed to examine the fragments of wood scattered on the ground. There were a few splinters inside the store on the floor, but they weren't what she would have expected if the door had been forced inward. When she looked up, John watched her with a knowing glint in his eye.

"The wood?" Mary asked.

He nodded. "We noticed it too. Since the noise wasn't enough to alert the animals or wake the family, we're inclined to think whoever broke in used quite a bit of force to pry it open with a knife or some other sharp instrument."

Mary tucked the information away and followed John and her sisters inside. Two more officers waited near the counter. One beckoned to John.

"Excuse me for a moment, ladies," John said. He motioned toward the rear of the store. "While you're waiting, if you wouldn't mind taking a look around...If you see anything unusual, call me, but try not to disturb it, and if you notice anything missing, make a note for me."

He withdrew a notepad and a pen and handed them to Elizabeth. Then he went to join the other officers at the counter.

Martha pointed toward the back. "Maybe we should start from there and work our way to the front."

"Good idea," Elizabeth said. Firming her chin, she plowed forward.

Things at the back of the store were not nearly as disordered as the front. Along the back wall, cubbies with dishes, candleholders, and a wide assortment of bric-a-brac were all neatly stacked, just as they had left them. Barrels with homemade soaps and embroidered towels stood like mute sentinels.

Mary gave the other displays and shelves a cursory glance and then gestured around her. "Everything here looks perfectly fine."

Elizabeth agreed and held up the notepad. "So far, I don't see anything to put on the list. Do either of you?"

They shook their heads, and Martha pointed to her right. "Should we check near the lamps and furniture?"

They nodded, and Martha led the way, but there too, the aisles looked neat and undisturbed.

"I don't get it," she said, jamming her hands on her hips. "If someone were going to break in, I figured they'd look back here. The only things nearer the front are my baked goods and some of the smaller stuff."

"Let's head that way," Elizabeth suggested, tucking the notepad under her arm.

Mary and Martha followed as Elizabeth led them toward the front, where most of the mess was scattered and where, as Martha had said, her baked goods were located. She had brought several boxes of fresh-baked muffins, pies, and cookies into the shop last night and left them, unopened, on a small table by the display case. She'd planned to arrange them in the case this morning. Only now, most of them were strewn on the floor. A few were trampled and the crumbs ground to powder. The rest remained intact, as though someone had simply dumped their entire stock onto the floor.

Martha scowled darkly at the mess. "Well, crumbs...what a waste." Then her lips pressed into a line, and she said nothing more.

Elizabeth lifted her hands. "It's a muddle, that's for sure, but does it look like there's anything missing?"

Mary looked around. The cash register did not appear to have been moved, nor had the shelves been emptied. "Not that I can see."

"Me neither," Martha said, her scowl deepening. "Which makes me ask—why did they bother?"

Elizabeth bit the eraser tip of her pencil hesitantly. "Maybe this was a prank? For all we know, it could have been a couple of kids who broke in on a dare and then chickened out and left."

"I don't know." Mary pinched her bottom lip and nudged one of the ruined cakes with her toe. "Whoever did this left a pretty big mess. That doesn't sound like a prank to me."

"Me neither." Martha bent and plucked a smooshed loaf of cranberry bread off the floor and held it up by the plastic wrapping. "But Elizabeth is right. Nothing was taken—"

Before she could finish, Mary squeezed her arm. "Martha, look."

Martha's gaze followed where Mary pointed to the blank space on the wall above the counter. "What is it?"

"Yes, what's wrong?" Elizabeth drew closer, her brows knitted in a frown.

Mary squeezed her eyes shut, afraid for a second that they were playing tricks on her. When she reopened them, she stared at the same blank space.

"It's my painting," she said, her voice a strangled whisper. She swallowed hard and tried again. "Someone has stolen my painting of Uncle Paul."

CHAPTER THIRTEEN

Martha squinted up at the blank spot on the wall where Mary's painting had hung. She pointed upward. "The nail is still there. Maybe it just fell."

Instantly, all three of them looked behind the table and saw the empty floor. Mary threw her hands up. "It's not here. Why on earth would anyone want to steal one of *my* paintings? I'm not famous. My work isn't even that good."

"Your work is wonderful," Martha fired back. She dropped the ruined loaf of cranberry bread into the trash can next to the cash register. "But I don't think that's why they took it."

"Took what?" John approached, his eyes questioning. "Did you ladies notice something missing?"

"My painting." Mary pointed to the wall. "It was hanging there yesterday. Now it's gone."

Elizabeth pulled John's notepad from her back pocket and handed it to him so he could jot down a few notes. He turned to Mary. "Was it valuable?"

"Only to me," she said. "It was a picture of the cemetery. When I hung it here in the store, I never imagined anyone would want to steal it."

"It was very lovely," Elizabeth said. "Mary used to do a lot of painting in her younger days. She's really talented."

Mary's cheeks flushed pink. "Thank you, Lizzie."

John clicked the top of his pen and motioned toward Mary. "So this painting—what can you tell me about it?"

Briefly, Mary explained what the painting had looked like and what had inspired her to create it. While she talked, John scribbled in the notepad. When she finished, he flipped the cover closed and slid it back into his pocket.

"Thank you, Mary. I'll add this to my report." He looked apologetically at Elizabeth. "Just so I cover all of my bases, there isn't any chance that someone else could have sold the painting without you knowing about it, right?"

Elizabeth shook her head. "My sisters and I run the store. We don't have any other hired help."

He nodded. "Okay. So what about the rest of the store? Did you see anything else missing?"

The three exchanged a glance and shook their heads in unison.

"All right then, I'll get this information back to the station."

"And look for my painting?" Mary asked.

He braced his hands on his hips. "We'll certainly try, but I should warn you, without a definite lead, there's not much chance we'll be able to recover your painting. Of course, if I hear anything, I'll let you know."

Mary looked disappointed, but she thanked him anyway. John motioned to Elizabeth, and the two stepped away to talk. Turning her back, Martha gestured to the mess on the floor with a sigh.

"Well, I suppose we'd best get started cleaning this up before the store opens."

"I'll get a broom." Mary started for the supply closet, then stopped and held up one finger. "Just a second—I forgot to tell John about the teapot."

Scurrying over to him, she pulled out her phone, swiped at the screen a few times, and gestured animatedly at it. Martha watched a second and then went to fetch the broom and a dustpan. It only took her a moment to sweep the largest part of the mess into a pile, but it broke her heart to see everything go into the trash.

"Martha, are you all right?" Done talking to John, Mary crossed to Martha and laid her hand on her shoulder. "Would you like me to finish cleaning this up?"

"I can do it," Martha insisted, raising her chin. "I just hate seeing all of my hard work go to waste."

Their eyes locked, and suddenly Martha realized that Mary felt exactly the same way about her painting. Neither one mentioned it, but the shared moment of understanding touched Martha's heart deeply. She gave Mary's hand upon her shoulder a squeeze and then went back to sweeping before Mary could see the tears gathering in her eyes.

Mary bent and picked up a clear plastic bag containing the remnants of a loaf of pumpkin bread. Holding it between her thumb and forefinger, she carried it over to the trash and then went back to the small table that had held the baked goods.

"Let me help you put that back." Martha reached for the end of the table, then froze and stared up at the wall. "Mary, wait, maybe we shouldn't move it."

Mary looked at the table, then at Martha uncertainly. "Why not? What's wrong?"

Martha waved her hand. "The table, it's pushed over toward the wall. Why do you suppose they did that?"

Mary shrugged. "I don't know. Maybe—" Suddenly she broke off, and her gaze drifted upward.

Martha nodded. "Uh-huh. They cleared the table off because they needed something to stand on."

"To get to my painting." Mary's head bobbed rapidly. "I'll get John."

Mary's words tumbled over and around themselves as she hurried to explain to John about the table. As she babbled, his eyes took on an interested gleam.

"All right, so it would appear that whoever broke in was specifically after that painting." He rubbed his chin thoughtfully. "Tell me again about this painting."

Mary explained the work again, this time including as many details as she could remember. "I also put our uncle in it," she said. "His name was Paul Classen. Unfortunately, we don't know all that much about him. He died before I was born. And Elizabeth and Martha were both very young." She frowned. "It was actually an accident that I had Uncle Paul standing on the hill overlooking the family plots," she said. "If Rafe Porter hadn't startled me…"

Rafe Porter. She narrowed her eyes, then shook her head. No, he wouldn't need the table. He knew where the ladder was. He'd gotten it and put it away for her the day she showed the painting to Della.

"Mary?" John looked at her questioningly.

"Sorry." She raised her hands helplessly. "Anyway, it was sort of a happy accident. Rafe startled me, and I jerked my hand up, creating a dark slash. When I got home, I changed it so it looked more like a shadow."

He nodded. "All right. So, apart from the painting itself, you have no idea why anyone would be interested enough to steal it?"

She shook her head. "It only has sentimental value, so unless the thief was family—"

She broke off and turned wide eyes to Elizabeth.

"Now, now." Elizabeth crossed to Mary quickly and laid her arm around her shoulders. "Let's not jump to any conclusions."

"Do you have a lot of family still living in Bird-in-Hand?" John asked.

"Some of them still live around here," Elizabeth said hesitantly. "But surely you don't think one of them could have been responsible?"

"You don't know what caused the rift between Paul Classen and your family, right?" he asked gently.

"But what would Mary's painting have to do with that?" she insisted.

John met her gaze, his eyes solemn. "I'm just saying it's possible someone doesn't *want* you to know. If that's the case, then any reminder of Paul, anything to do with him at all, might stir up some old fear and resentment."

Though her pursed lips indicated she didn't like it, Elizabeth nodded, showing she understood.

John moved off to speak to the other officers, who were preparing to leave. When he returned, he motioned around the store.

"Okay, that's all we can do for now. I can stay and help you get this mess cleaned up, if you'd like."

Mary shook her head.

"I'm sure we can manage. Thank you anyway, John. We appreciate your help this morning."

He stepped toward the door. "What about the lock? Do you have someone who can fix it?"

Elizabeth looked to Mary.

"I'll give Bill a call," she said, giving her sister's arm a pat. "If he can't do it, I'm sure he can recommend someone who can come out this afternoon."

John nodded and turned for the door reluctantly. "Okay, well, let me know if I can be of any help."

Sunlight glinted off the glass as he opened the door and stepped outside. Mary turned back to the mess on the floor with a sigh.

"Well, I suppose we'd better get busy helping Martha." She frowned. "Where is she, by the way?"

"I think I saw her taking out the trash." Elizabeth pointed to the empty trash can.

Mary tsked. "Poor Martha. She was pretty upset seeing all her hard work go to waste."

"Well then, let's hurry and get the rest of this swept up before she gets back," Elizabeth said, reaching for the broom.

While Elizabeth swept, Mary put on a pair of work gloves and scooped the larger items off the floor. Something shiny caught her eye, and she dropped to her hands and knees to retrieve it.

"Say, what's this?" She squinted to study the small piece of dark blue plastic nestled in her palm. It was half-moon shaped and contained one hole slightly off center. "It almost looks like a piece of a button. What do you think?"

She held it toward Elizabeth, who took it between her thumb and forefinger, studied it, then flipped it over and studied the other side. "You're probably right. It looks like a button off of someone's jacket."

The doorbell chimed, and Martha entered with a fresh trash bag in her hands. When she spotted them, she dropped the bag onto the counter and crossed over to them. "What are you two looking at?"

Elizabeth showed her. Martha grunted as she studied it, then held it out to Mary.

As she took the button back, Mary's heart fluttered with excitement. "Do you think maybe this fell off of whoever broke in here last night?"

"It's possible, I suppose," Elizabeth said hesitantly, "but, Mary, so many people pass through here every day. There's no way we could prove that particular button belongs to"—she spread her hands wide—"whoever did this."

Martha nodded her agreement. "She's right, Mary. Who knows how long that thing has been there? All it tells us is that we may need to do a better job of sweeping."

Mary closed the button tightly in her hand. "You could be right, but I swept last night, and I'm sure I swept this area."

Rather than toss the broken button into the trash, she tucked it into her pocket and then bent to finish with the cleanup. For now, she'd concentrate on getting the store ready to open, but more than likely, she'd spend the rest of the day looking at people's jackets for a missing or broken button.

CHAPTER FOURTEEN

Mary's conversation with the people at the bank where Della used to work did not turn up any new leads to her whereabouts. She hid a small smile as she watched Bill put the finishing touches on the store's new keyless entry. Bill had come over as promised to make the repairs after he got done with work that day. He gave the keypad one final polish with his handkerchief then, satisfied with the job, he closed the door and slid the cloth back into his back pocket.

Mary shoved her thoughts aside as he straightened and pushed his ratty baseball cap off his forehead with his thumb.

"Okay, that ought to do it. You now have a commercial-grade keyless entry. Are you sure you remember how to program the PIN numbers?"

She nodded. "Yes. Thank you so much, Bill. We really appreciate you coming over to take care of this, especially since you've already put in a long day." She pointed at the keypad. "If you'll give me your invoice, I'll get Martha to write you a check for your work."

He was shaking his head even before she finished. "Don't worry about that, Mary. I was just glad I could help out a friend." He wiped the WD-40 from his hands, wadded up the paper towel, and shoved it into his back pocket. "And we are friends, right?"

"Of course," she said quickly, "but you have to at least let us pay for the parts. A true friend wouldn't take advantage of you."

He chuckled and put up his hands in defeat. "All right, I'll email you something later this evening."

"Sounds good." She blew out a breath, glad to have the awkward moment behind them.

Bill braced his hands on his hips as he looked around the store. "Anything else you need me to do? I'd be happy to take a look at the windows for you, if you'd like, just to make sure those are secure."

Mary followed his gaze to the windows mounted alongside the door. They were not new but not in need of repair, at least, not any that she knew. She shook her head. "I couldn't ask you to do that, Bill."

"Why not? It'll only take a minute."

He started that way, then looked back at her, waiting. Finally, she agreed with a smile. "Well, I suppose if you wouldn't mind…"

"Not at all." He crossed to the windows, checking each one before giving a satisfied nod. "All clear here. Looks like you have some pretty good quality locks."

"Yeah, my parents paid a little extra when they had the windows replaced, but I'm glad they took care of it so my sisters and I don't have to."

"That was good planning on their part." He pointed at the window above their heads. "That one's too high for anyone to reach without a ladder, so I don't think it'll be a problem. Any more windows in the back?"

Mary walked him slowly around the store. In fact, it felt more like a stroll than a check of their security. When they finished, Bill took off his tool belt and laid it gently on top of the counter.

"Okay, I'd say you're all set."

"Thanks, Bill. I know I'll rest better tonight, and I'm pretty sure my sisters will too."

"So will I." Their gazes met, and then his drifted upward, to the blank spot on the wall above the cash register. "Any word on your missing painting?"

He remembered. Even more importantly, he sounded concerned.

Mary's heart warmed with gratitude. "Not yet, but I'm hopeful something will turn up. Not that my painting was valuable or anything, but I sure would like to have it back."

"That's understandable. I'd be upset too, if I'd spent that much time working on something."

She smiled and shoved her hands into the pockets of her jeans while she fought not to fidget.

Bill cleared his throat. "So, do you have any plans for dinner? I was thinking about grabbing a quick bite on my way home from work."

"Actually, Martha probably already has supper about ready," Mary said, and then added, "but you're welcome to join us, if you'd like."

Bill's gaze dropped to his work clothes. Here and there, flecks of sawdust clung to his shirt, and there was a dark circle on his jeans where a drop of WD-40 had splattered. He brushed at the sawdust, then looked up at her. "Are you sure? Maybe I should run home and clean up first."

"Don't be silly," she chided with a smile. "Mama and Daddy never snubbed their noses at good, hardworking folks, and neither do we. Besides, it's the least we can do for you in exchange for fixing our door."

He looked pleased by her answer. His brown eyes twinkled as he agreed, and then he followed her up the hill to the house.

Tink met them at the door, her tail wagging furiously as she jumped up to greet Bill. Instead of pushing her away, he stooped to rub her behind the ears.

Mary watched a moment. Brian never had time for animals. Tink knew it and had always stayed as far away from him as possible. Bill, on the other hand...

He gave Tink one last pat and rose.

Mary pointed down the hall. "I'm sure you remember where the bathroom is. You can wash up in there while I go and help Martha and Elizabeth get supper on the table."

She stood watching him as he swung toward the bathroom, his broad shoulders making the hallway seem narrow.

Behind her, Elizabeth cleared her throat.

Mary spun to face her sister. "How long have you been standing there?"

Elizabeth's eyes sparkled as she swept her hand toward the wall behind her. "It's a dining room...where we dine...and it's almost time for supper. Where else would I be?"

"Right." Mary pulled her composure around her tightly and sidestepped her sister on the way to the table. "We've got one extra for supper. Would you mind letting Martha know while I set the table?"

She cringed as Elizabeth's chuckle drifted toward the kitchen. She'd have to be more careful about letting her thoughts run away with her, at least in front of her sisters. She was putting the last plate in place when Bill appeared.

She tugged out a chair. "You can sit here."

She circled the table and took a seat across from him just as Martha appeared.

"Hello, Bill. I'm glad you could join us." She set a bowl of fresh peas on the table and then went to give Bill a hug. "Elizabeth tells me you were able to get the lock on the store fixed."

He nodded. "Yep. You shouldn't have any more trouble, except, have you thought about having a security system installed?"

"We've never had to think about it before," Elizabeth said, following behind Martha and holding a platter stacked with rolls. "But I suppose we'll have to consider it now."

Bill gestured toward the kitchen. "Can I help you in there?"

"We've got it," Martha said, shooing him back toward his seat.

"I'm helping," Elizabeth called cheerfully from the kitchen. She emerged again carrying a serving platter laden with steaming potatoes.

"Here, let me help you with that," Bill said. Rising rapidly, he relieved her of the platter and set it on the table next to the peas. "This looks delicious. I haven't had a home-cooked meal in ages."

"Well then, you're in for a treat. Martha is an excellent cook," Mary said.

"You're not so bad either," Elizabeth said. Her gaze flew to Bill. "You should try her coconut cream pie. It's to die for."

"Don't be silly," Mary said, fighting rising warmth in her cheeks. "Pie is easy."

"Not for me," Elizabeth insisted. Behind her, Martha entered with a roasted chicken. They sat, Elizabeth said grace, and they started passing the serving dishes.

Mary found herself enjoying Bill's easy humor. He seemed completely at ease with her sisters, something Brian had never achieved.

She frowned and speared a small piece of potato. One day she would stop comparing every other male in the world to Brian.

Martha said suddenly, "We bought these dishes from Della, didn't we?"

Mary's gaze dropped to the floral-printed plates Della had purchased from a garage sale. Elizabeth had liked them and bought the entire set.

"I've been thinking a lot about Della." Martha set her glass aside and pressed her napkin to her lips. "Do either of you remember where she bought the teapot she sold to Mary?"

"Where is it, anyway?" Elizabeth asked. "I never got a good look at it."

Mary rose to fetch the teapot from the office and brought it to the table.

Bill leaned forward in his chair for a better look. "It *is* pretty, but I had no idea those things could be valuable."

"They can be, depending on the age and make." Elizabeth set her fork down and tapped the lid. "We don't know enough about this one to be sure yet." She turned to Mary. "Speaking of which, what did John tell you when you showed him the Facebook post?"

"He wasn't convinced there was a connection," Mary said, placing the teapot in the china cabinet before returning to her seat. "But he had me text him the picture and told me he'd be in touch if he learned anything new."

"You still haven't answered my question." Finished with her supper, Martha pushed aside her plate and motioned toward the teapot. "Where did Della say she bought it?"

"A garage sale," Mary said.

"But which one?"

"It'd be easy enough to find out," Mary said. "We could call Linda or one of the others. I'm sure they could tell us. I have their numbers in my phone."

She rose, and Bill rose with her.

"I should probably be going." He looked at Martha. "Thank you so much for supper. The chicken was excellent."

Mary watched as Martha and Elizabeth hurried over to bid him goodbye. With her sisters on either side, he walked to the door. When he reached it, he stopped.

"Let me know if you all decide to look into an alarm system. I'll be happy to give you a hand choosing one."

Elizabeth and Martha watched her expectantly, but Mary kept her mouth clamped shut stubbornly. They wanted her to invite him back, to say she would be in touch, but even knowing that, the words refused to come.

Bill cleared his throat, and he said one final goodbye. Mary lifted her hand in a feeble wave. The moment the door closed behind him, Elizabeth whirled and jammed her hands onto her hips.

"What was that all about? I thought you and he—"

"I'll call Linda," Mary said. She gestured toward the clock. "It's only seven thirty, so I'm sure it'll be all right."

Searching for her phone gave her the excuse she needed to duck out of sight. Behind her, Martha's animated voice mingled with Elizabeth's, but Mary didn't care. She and Bill were good friends, and she wasn't going to mess that up with unwanted expectations, no matter what her sisters thought.

CHAPTER FIFTEEN

After a busy day at the store, Mary laid her apron over the counter and locked the door at exactly five o'clock. As she had hoped, Linda remembered where Della had purchased the teapot and was able to give them fairly detailed directions. Martha volunteered to drive as the sisters struck out for the home of Selma and Frank Mueller. She pulled her car around and waited while Elizabeth and Mary climbed inside.

"You sure you know where we're going?" Martha asked.

Mary clicked her seat belt into place and then patted her pocket. "I have the directions right here. Linda said she remembered exactly where Della bought that teapot, because the owner was so chatty."

"Good," Martha said, shifting the car into DRIVE.

"Selma Mueller." Elizabeth repeated the name Linda had given them slowly. "Seems like I know that name from somewhere." She shrugged. "Maybe it'll come to me when I see what she looks like."

The Muellers' home wasn't too far from their farm. Martha navigated the roads easily, and in less than ten minutes, they were pulling up outside a pretty, two-story colonial home. It was painted a cheery blue, but the white trim and lofty columns kept it dignified. Black shutters accented the tall windows while a row of neatly trimmed hedges lined a winding brick path all the way up to the door.

Mary knocked and then stepped back alongside her sisters.

"Do you think they're home?" Elizabeth whispered.

Her question was answered a second later when the door swung open, and a short, trim woman with blond hair, graying at the temples, greeted them with a smile that instantly struck Mary as familiar.

The woman's gaze ran over all three of them curiously. "Can I help you?"

When Mary didn't move, Martha urged her forward with her elbow.

"Uh, Mrs. Mueller?"

"Yes, I'm Selma Mueller."

Mary placed her hand on her chest. "My name is Mary Baxter, and these are my sisters, Elizabeth Classen and Martha Watts. You may have heard of us. We own the Secondhand Blessings store across town."

Lines of puzzlement creased Selma's brow until Mary mentioned the store. Instantly, the lines cleared, and she smiled.

"Oh, you mean the old barn? Yes, I know that place." She opened the door a little wider. "Would you like to come in?"

Mary followed as her sisters trailed Selma into a wide, stately hallway. The wood floors were polished to a high gleam, with not a single seam to mar the expansive space. Selma's shoes clicked softly as she led them into a small yet elegant room that split off the hall. Inside, the room was appointed with lovely plum drapes that pooled on the floor. Beautifully framed family photos decorated the walls, and an elegant bronze fan that looked more like a piece of art than an appliance gently stirred the air and kept the room from feeling stuffy.

Selma led them to a long leather settee. "Can I get you ladies something to drink?"

Mary, Martha, and Elizabeth sank side by side on the couch. Were it not for Selma's smile, Mary might have felt as though they'd been called to task for something. All three shook their heads.

"No, thank you," Martha said. "I believe we're fine."

Selma perched on a wine-colored rocker, the wood trim of which framed her hair perfectly. "All right then, what can I do for you?"

Apparently, Martha felt as uncomfortable as Mary. She stammered through the reason for their visit and then fell silent with her lips pressed into a thin line.

"The garage sale?" Selma looked genuinely confused. Her hand rose to finger the pearl necklace at her throat. "Yes, I sold several things at that, including a silver teapot. A lady bought it. Oh, what was her name?" She tapped her forehead, struggling to recall the information.

"Actually," Mary said, leaning forward on the settee, "we're more interested in the teapot. Could you tell us where it came from?"

Selma's hand fell to her lap. "To be honest, I really couldn't say."

The sisters shared a glance. She couldn't *say*, or she couldn't remember?

"I see I've confused you." Selma rose and paced. The click of her heels was muted on the throw rug at the center of the room but grew louder as she approached one of the tall windows and peered out. "My husband, Frank"—she glanced at them over her shoulder and looked back out the window—"had a heart attack recently."

"We're very sorry to hear that," Elizabeth said. "Is he all right?"

"He's better, but it will be some time before he can come home." She sighed heavily. "Currently he's in a nursing home, where he'll stay until he recovers. Unfortunately, the cost for his care has been quite expensive." She motioned around the large house. "I thought maybe now would be a good time to get rid of a few things, maybe empty out some clutter in case…well…in case it becomes necessary to look for a smaller place."

Mary was feeling worse by the second. The last thing these people needed was for the three of them to show up asking questions. She squirmed uncomfortably.

Selma shook her head wryly. "Not that we weren't considering downsizing before Frank's heart attack. This big house, and all these stairs…" She sighed again. "Well, let's just say his health issues have kind of expedited our decision."

She moved away from the window and returned to the rocking chair, where she sat, her ankles crossed gracefully. "Anyway, the teapot was one of the many things I dug out of the attic."

"Do you remember where you got it?" Mary asked.

Selma shook her head. "It wasn't mine. I assumed it was something Frank had collected on one of his many wanderings. He used to travel a lot for work," she explained. "He was a claims adjuster for a large insurance agency before he retired—industrial accidents mostly, but also some natural disasters and a few smaller claims. Some years, he was gone for months at a time."

"Sounds like a difficult way of life," Martha said.

Selma nodded. "It could be. He missed a lot of 'firsts' when our children were growing up. But then he'd come home with some fantastic story of the places he'd gone and the things he'd seen, and we would find a way to move on." She motioned to Mary. "Frank used to like bringing us gifts, especially when he'd been gone a long time."

"So, if the teapot was a gift, why do you suppose he never gave it to you?" she asked.

Selma smoothed a wrinkle in her skirt. "As I said, our life together wasn't always easy. We had a few rough patches along the way, but we always managed to work them out."

"Every married couple experiences something like that," Martha said. Mary was glad for the look of gratitude she read in Selma's gaze.

After a moment, Selma lifted her chin. "I should tell you that I don't think Frank ever intended the teapot to be a gift. I stumbled upon it in the attic one Christmas while I was hunting for decorations. I told him I thought it was beautiful, but he refused to let me display it. He insisted we keep it stored in the attic. It became quite a bone of contention between us, one I was only too happy to get rid of when I sold it at the garage sale."

Her eyes widened, and she snapped her fingers. "You know, I *do* remember the lady's name. The one who bought that teapot? It was Della...uh...Bradford. That's it. She was an older woman with short graying hair. And very energetic, if I remember correctly." She laughed lightly. "I guess she would have to be to get out to the sale so early. She and the other three ladies she was with were here an hour before the sale even began. Lucky for Della too, because I had several people ask me about the teapot. I had to tell them it was already sold." Her gaze cleared and settled on Elizabeth. "What is all this about? Is she in some kind of trouble? Why are you looking for her?"

"Oh no, it's nothing like that," Elizabeth said. She stiffened, and when she spoke, it seemed to Mary that she formed each word carefully. "It's just that her apartment was broken into recently, and we thought maybe it was the teapot the intruder was after."

Selma looked even more confused. "Why? Was it valuable or something?" She rose and crossed to the window again. "I would never have sold it if I had known. Frank never told me where it came from, so I just assumed . . ."

Mary rose and crossed to stand in front of her. Someone had to set things straight, and she intended to do just that before Elizabeth worried Selma even more by blurting out that Della had disappeared.

"We have no idea what the teapot is worth. It was just a hunch, so we thought we would ask you what you knew about it, that's all."

Selma plucked nervously at her bottom lip. "I—I suppose if you want to know any more, you'll have to speak to my husband. He's the only one who could tell you for sure where he got it."

"Thank you," Martha said quietly. "We won't take up any more of your time."

The time had come to leave. Still, with something about Selma Mueller tugging at Mary's memory, she hesitated.

"Was there something else?" Selma asked.

"Um..." Mary squinted, trying hard to place exactly what it was about her that seemed so familiar. "I'm sorry, but have we ever met?"

Selma's puzzled frown cleared. "Actually, my husband and I do have some connections to your family."

"Really?" Martha tilted her head. "How so?"

"Well," Selma said, her smile widening, "we knew one of your uncles quite well. It was many years ago, of course, but we were very close once."

"Our uncle?" Curiosity gleamed in Elizabeth's eyes as she rose to stand. "Do you mind if we ask which one?"

Selma turned from the window and dropped her hand to her side. "Not at all. It was Paul Classen."

CHAPTER SIXTEEN

You knew our uncle Paul?" Mary's heart pattered with excitement at this bit of good news. Perhaps Selma would be able to tell them what had happened all those years ago to cause such a rift between him and the rest of the Classen family.

Selma's smile faded. She moved back to the rocking chair and sat. Mary and Elizabeth moved with her and reclaimed their seats next to Martha.

"My husband and Paul were good friends before I met Frank. They were also a few years older." She laid her hand on her chest. "We were still in high school when Frank and I started dating, and we married when he graduated. I actually got my GED a few years later."

High school sweethearts.

Mary's breathing hitched painfully. She clasped her hands together in her lap. Now was not the time to think about Brian. "Um...d-do you mind telling us what you remember about him? Uncle P-Paul, I mean."

Martha glanced at her sharply, and Mary read the question in her eyes. *What is wrong with you?* She averted her eyes from Martha's gaze and focused on Selma.

"Well, let's see...he was a nice boy, very generous and kind, a year behind Frank in school. He had kind of a wild streak, if I remember correctly."

"A wild streak?" Elizabeth leaned forward, as though she hoped to catch every word the moment it fell from Selma's mouth.

"Well, only compared to the other Classen children," Selma said. "They were all so focused and proper, especially when it came to running the farm." She paused. "And wasn't the family Amish or something?"

"Mennonite," Martha clarified.

Selma nodded. "I thought I remembered seeing them in plain dress. Anyway, Paul was different. He told Frank on more than one occasion that he didn't want to spend his life farming. I think that was hard on the rest of the family. They all felt like he was saying their life wasn't good enough for him."

Could that be all it was? Was Paul's desire to leave farming behind the wedge it had taken to open the rift? Mary leaned forward and gripped her knees tightly. "What else do you remember?"

"Oh, not much, I'm afraid. We lost touch with him after Frank and I married, and years later, we heard he'd been killed in a car wreck." Selma thought for a moment and then snapped her fingers. "You know, I think I have a photo of Paul and Frank together. If you'll wait, I'll see if I can find it."

Martha and Elizabeth were already nodding, so Mary added her agreement. "That would be wonderful, Selma. Thank you."

She hurried out and returned a few minutes later carrying a tattered photo album with faded gold lettering. She huffed to catch her breath as she laid it on the coffee table in front of them. "I think this is the right album. It belongs to Frank.

Neither of us has looked at it in years, but I didn't have the heart to toss it out. Some things just can't be replaced."

She flipped open the cover, skimming past several pages and finally slowing when she reached a few that showed a striking young man in uniform. Her eyes misted as she tapped the photo. "That's Frank. He must have been around twenty years old or so when this was taken. I remember being swept away by how handsome he was."

The same could be said for the first time Mary had laid eyes on Brian. She squirmed in her chair and tried not to think about him. "Frank was in the army?"

Selma nodded. "He served for almost ten years. In fact, we moved around quite a bit when we first married. But then our children came along, and Frank decided he didn't want the military life for them. When he got the job as an adjuster, we settled here to be close to family."

"That's certainly understandable. I bet the family was glad to have you nearby."

Selma flipped the page and then gave a small, satisfied grunt. "Ah, here it is. I knew I remembered seeing it. Frank is a junior in this picture, so Paul would have been a sophomore."

She turned the book around and pointed to a picture of two young men standing side by side. The shorter of the two was obviously Frank. Mary's eyes were drawn to the taller man.

Paul Classen looked exactly like a younger version of their father. He had the same smiling blue eyes and sandy-blond hair, but he was much lankier of frame.

"The resemblance is incredible," Elizabeth whispered.

"I was thinking the same thing," Martha said.

Selma shot them a puzzled frown. "You didn't know your uncle?"

"He died before I was born, and my sisters were very young," Mary said, hoping Selma didn't press further.

She didn't. Instead, she slid the photo out of the album and handed it to Mary. "You can keep it if you'd like."

Mary held the picture reverently. "Are you sure? I mean, it has your husband in it too."

She laughed and waved her hand. "I have lots of photos of Frank. Please, take it with my blessing."

"Thank you."

Mary handed the photo to Martha, who studied it a moment before slipping it carefully into her purse.

Fighting an attack of nerves, Mary licked her lips, hesitant to ask which nursing home Frank lived in. But they had to figure out what happened to Della, and the teapot was their only lead. She sucked in a breath and blew it out slowly.

"Selma, do you think Frank would mind if we stopped by to ask him about the teapot?"

"Not at all." She closed the photo album and laid it on the coffee table. "He enjoys having visitors. In fact, I bet he'd love meeting Paul's nieces." She scribbled the name of one of the local nursing homes on a piece of paper and handed it to Mary. "The best time to visit is from eight to around eleven thirty in the morning. He plays Scrabble with some of the other patients in the afternoon and then usually hits the hay around eight thirty or nine. Ever since his heart attack, he likes to go to bed early."

She gave them his room number and then walked them to the door. "Good luck," she said as they made their way outside.

"Let me know if there is anything else I can do for you. I'll be glad to help."

All three thanked her and then returned to the car, but Mary was still perplexed as she reached for her seat belt and locked it into place.

"Something bothering you?" Martha asked, turning the key in the ignition.

"It's just that I can't seem to place her," Mary said absently.

"Who? Selma?" Elizabeth asked, settling onto the back seat.

Mary gave a low grunt. "She looked so familiar. I was surprised when she opened the door, but I can't for the life of me think where I know her from, unless..." She tapped her temple, thinking. "Well, I suppose it will come to me."

Mary couldn't get the puzzle out of her head all the way home. Selma had looked familiar to her, but even after wracking her brain every which way, she couldn't figure out why. Added to the nagging worry over Della, Mary knew she couldn't spend another evening twiddling her thumbs.

She scooted out of the car the moment Martha parked, and jogged up the steps toward the house. "How about if I drive into town and grab us something from the diner?"

Elizabeth pushed the car door closed and then glanced at Martha. "It's been a long day, and I think that sounds great. What do you say, Martha?"

Martha rounded the car and pressed her finger to her lips. "Hmm, I was planning to have the leftover lasagna tonight, but it'll keep till tomorrow. With the added bonus of not having to cook for supper after the potluck at church."

"That's perfect." Elizabeth waved to Mary. "Go for it!"

Mary climbed into her car and drove the short distance to the Bird-in-Hand Bakery and Café. Her watch said they were approaching closing, but hopefully they could stay open long enough for her to order three sandwiches.

The doorbell chimed as she slipped inside. She made her way to the counter where a fresh-faced young woman wearing a bright red apron greeted her with a smile.

"Good evening. Welcome to the Bird-in-Hand Bakery and Café."

"Thank you." Mary fidgeted uncomfortably. "I'm not too late to order some sandwiches to go, am I? I know it's getting close to closing time."

The young woman's eyes drifted to the clock on the wall to her right. Mary cringed. It was much closer to six than she'd realized.

She backed up a step and waved toward the door. "You know what...I don't want to keep you. I'll just get something somewhere else."

"It's really all right," the young woman assured her. "Let me ask the kitchen staff. I'm sure we could whip something up for you."

"Or...," someone interrupted.

Mary whirled toward the voice. She hadn't seen anyone when she came in and only now realized she wasn't alone in the café.

Rafe Porter raised a paper bag stamped with the café's logo. "You could share my sandwich with me. How does a chicken, spinach, and feta panini sound?"

"It sounds wonderful. I'm sure you'll enjoy it." Mary turned toward the counter again, holding her breath as Rafe's footsteps sounded behind her.

Mary resisted the urge to sweep her gaze heavenward. Instead, she turned and faced him head on.

"Look, I'm here to get sandwiches for me and my sisters, so I appreciate the offer, but…" She shrugged.

He looked down at the bag and then at her. "Well, all right then."

The young woman returned from the kitchen. "The staff says you're in time, if you like chicken salad. We have some of that left from today."

"That would be just fine." Mary sighed in relief. "I'll take three chicken salad sandwiches, please, one on rye, one on Asiago cheese, and one on whole wheat."

Rafe was still standing there after she paid for the sandwiches. "Look, we seem to have gotten off on the wrong foot. Did I do something to upset you?"

She forced her stance to soften and pushed her hands into her pockets. "No."

"Well then, is this about the painting?"

He knew it had been stolen? "M-my painting?" she stammered.

He nodded. "You're still mad that I ruined it."

"No, I…" She swallowed hard. "You didn't ruin it."

Rafe grinned—a knock-your-socks-off kind of grin that triggered a half-dozen alarm bells in Mary's head. "Sooo, you're not mad at me, and I didn't ruin your painting. How about we eat our sandwiches together in the park, and your sisters can wait a few more minutes for their supper?"

Mary looked at him, dumbfounded. He really thought he was all that? "Thank you, but no," she said. "Martha and Elizabeth are waiting for me."

Confusion clouded his gaze—and it was precisely that look that solidified the decision in her head. He wasn't used to being turned down, like someone else she'd known—someone who'd broken her heart. He'd opened his mouth to keep talking when she noticed his jacket.

He was missing a button. A blue button.

"Mary?"

She must have been staring. She stammered something—she hardly knew what—took the bag the young woman handed her, and whirled out the door.

CHAPTER SEVENTEEN

The clock on the wall in the living room ticked quietly. Normally, Martha wasn't even aware of it, but with the only other sound being the rustle of the newspaper Elizabeth was reading, she couldn't help but tune to it. She twisted her wrist to read her watch. It was only two minutes slower than the clock.

Drumming her fingers against the arms of her chair, she said, "I'm getting hungry."

Elizabeth glanced over the top of the newspaper at her and shrugged. "Mary will be here soon. Besides, she hasn't been gone that long."

She ducked back behind the paper. Martha sighed. She went to her purse and pulled out the photo of Uncle Paul and Frank Mueller that Selma had given them. Their uncle certainly was handsome, in a lanky Paul Newman sort of way.

She returned to her chair and snapped on the lamp. After a moment, she said, "Elizabeth, did Selma say how Uncle Paul and Frank met?"

Elizabeth lowered the paper. "She said they were friends before she knew them, so I assume they must have gone to school together."

"More than likely." Martha studied the picture and then looked up again. "Hey, have you heard from Uncle George?"

"No, but I've left him several messages. I'm sure he'll call when he has a moment." She tilted her head and eyed Martha curiously. "What's wrong?"

Martha puffed out a breath and laid the photo on the end table. "I don't know. I suppose I'm just worried."

"About Uncle Paul?"

"And Della. Her disappearance has me rattled." She rose and crossed to the door. "I'm going to make myself a cup of tea. Would you like one?"

"Sure." Elizabeth followed Martha to the kitchen. "I *do* think it's interesting that both of these mysteries have a common connection."

"The Muellers?"

"Yes." Elizabeth reached into the cupboard for two cups while Martha filled a kettle with water.

"I do too. I'm glad Mary asked about speaking to Frank." She turned on a burner on the stove and turned to rest her hip against the counter. "I think we should plan on doing that, maybe Monday?"

Indecision marred Elizabeth's features. "There's a woman coming to look at some furniture Monday. I would call her, but she's traveling from West Chester." She frowned and put the cups down. "Besides, someone has to run the store. Maybe you and Mary can go."

Martha shrugged and turned back to the kettle. "What did you make of all that business with the teapot?"

"It's strange, for sure." Elizabeth took out the cream and sugar bowl and set them next to the cups. "Why would Frank purchase something like that and never do anything with it?"

"We could ask him, I suppose."

The kettle whistled. Martha lifted a bright yellow box and showed it to Elizabeth. "Chamomile okay?"

"Perfect."

She dropped a tea bag in each cup and then filled them with water. When she finished, she replaced the kettle on the stove, and she and Elizabeth carried their cups to the table, but instead of sitting down, Martha crossed to a drawer and took out a pencil and a piece of paper.

"What's that for?" Elizabeth asked as Martha returned to the table.

"For making a list." She pulled out a chair across from her sister and sat. "I think I should write down all of the questions we would like to ask Frank so we don't forget anything."

"Good idea." Elizabeth laced her fingers around her cup. "I, for one, would like to know how he and Uncle Paul met."

Martha scribbled the question down. "I'd also like to know if he remembers what happened between Uncle Paul and the family."

"Good." Elizabeth took a sip from her cup. "And what about the teapot? Are you going to ask him where he got it?"

"Definitely." Martha jotted it under the questions about Uncle Paul. "What else?"

Both she and Elizabeth drank their tea while they thought. After a moment, Martha pushed aside her cup and twiddled the pencil against the tabletop. "Maybe Mary will be able to think of some things we should ask him."

Elizabeth agreed, and then arched one eyebrow. "Speaking of Mary…what do you think is going on with her and Bill?"

"They like each other well enough, I suppose." Martha eyed her sister curiously. "Why?"

Elizabeth lowered her gaze and fiddled with the handle of her cup. "I saw her talking to Rafe Porter the other day."

"You did? Where?"

"In the store. He was helping her with her painting."

"Nothing wrong with that, right? He seems like a nice guy."

"Do you think so?"

Martha narrowed her eyes and studied the worried expression on her sister's face. "You don't?"

"It's just…" Elizabeth pushed her cup away and clasped her hands. "He reminds me an awful lot of Brian."

"You're kidding." Martha frowned. "I didn't realize you knew Rafe that well."

"I don't. It's more of a gut feeling." She shook her head. "I know I shouldn't draw hasty conclusions. I'm just worried about Mary."

Martha reached out to pat Elizabeth's hand. "We're going to have to let her make her own decisions."

"I know, but I don't want to see her hurt again. Bill is kind. Sweet. Rafe, on the other hand…"

"He's certainly handsome."

"So was Brian," Elizabeth huffed, and then her lips curved in a knowing smile. "Say what you like, Martha Watts. You're just as worried about her as I am."

"Oh, go on," Martha said, shooing her with wave. She didn't say it, but Elizabeth was right. She *was* worried about their youngest sister. Mary had made some mistakes in the past, but she was older now. Surely she had learned from them… hadn't she?

CHAPTER EIGHTEEN

Mary fingered the broken button she'd found in the store. Flipping it over, she examined the back side for a long moment, and then finally ended up slipping it back into the drawer of her nightstand.

It wasn't the same button.

The buttons on Rafe's jacket were a lighter blue. She'd realized that last night after she'd raced home to check but still felt compelled to look again this morning. Why? Would she forever be leery of any man who even remotely reminded her of her ex-husband?

The bedsprings complained as she stood and reached for her robe. Whatever her reservations were regarding Rafe, they had nothing to do with her missing painting.

Thinking of her painting reminded her of the day before. The three of them attended the first-Sunday hymn sing at their church, followed by a potluck dinner on the grounds—featuring delicious *varenyky* of all kinds. Afterward, they'd visited Rachel Fischer and her family. She told them about a quilt auction she'd recently been to in Lancaster. Rachel had donated two gorgeous quilts to be auctioned, and the proceeds went to local charities. Mary walked to the window and looked out, letting her fancy take flight. What if her paintings were someday auctioned off at high prices to help feed children or teach them to read?

Startled from her dreams by a knock at her door, she crossed to answer. Martha stood in the hall, a cup of steaming coffee in her hands.

She held the cup toward Mary. "Sorry. I hope I didn't wake you."

Mary stifled a yawn as she accepted the coffee and shuffled back toward her bed. "You didn't wake me. I've been up for a while."

Martha crossed to smooth the covers and then sat down on the bed. "Something bothering you? I mean besides being worried about Della."

Rather than answer, Mary took a sip of her coffee while she organized her thoughts. Finally, she told Martha about the button and her suspicions regarding Rafe. Martha appeared surprised to learn that she'd kept the button, but she listened quietly. When Mary finished, she sat down at the vanity and set her coffee aside.

"I don't know, Martha. Maybe I'm not being fair to Rafe. Maybe I'm blaming him for my own insecurities."

"That's understandable, you know."

Mary stared at her sister in surprise. She expected sympathy from Elizabeth, but Martha tended to be more pragmatic.

Martha laughed. "I know what you're thinking, but it's true, Mary. You've been through a lot. It will take time for you to learn to trust yourself again. Just don't lose sight of the fact that you're older now and much wiser than you were when you married Brian." She rose and clasped Mary's shoulder. "And more importantly you were a great mother to Michael and Jennifer. They appreciate and love you, no matter what. Let that be enough."

Hearing such tenderness from Martha instantly brought tears to Mary's eyes. She nodded her thanks and then reached for a tissue.

"Anyway, that's not why I came up here," Martha said.

Though she turned away, Mary glimpsed the tears glistening in her sister's eyes. It warmed her heart even more, but she wouldn't embarrass Martha by pointing it out. She sniffled and tossed the balled-up tissue in the trash. "So why did you come?"

"I wanted to see what your plans are for today. Elizabeth and I talked Saturday night about going to see Frank Mueller. She has an appointment and can't leave the store, but she hoped maybe you and I could go. Are you up to it?"

Mary nodded eagerly. "You think he'll be able to tell us something?"

"Only one way to find out." Martha stood and motioned to the closet. "Get dressed and meet me downstairs."

Mary gulped the rest of her coffee and then hurried to the bathroom to wash. Thinking about her sister's words made her smile. Thinking about working with her sister to figure out what had happened to Della kept the smile in place as she darted down the stairs to the kitchen. Odd, after all these years—a good kind of odd—to be feeling like they had things in common, goals that they were both working toward, not only in the situation with Della but in the greater goal of making the store successful again.

Martha met her with a piece of toast and more coffee in a travel mug.

"Where's Elizabeth?" Mary asked around a mouthful of toast.

"She's already down at the store. I told her we would head back as soon as we finish up with Frank Mueller and give her a full report."

Holding the toast between her teeth, Mary jammed her arms into a light sweater and followed Martha out to her car.

"So were you able to find the address of the nursing home where Selma told us Frank is staying?" she asked as she climbed into the car.

Martha patted her purse. "I've already typed the address into my phone. Would you mind pulling up the navigation for me?"

Mary pushed her coffee mug into a cup holder and gobbled the rest of her toast before digging into Martha's purse.

"Password?" she asked when she found the phone.

"Gingerbread." Martha put the car in REVERSE and backed carefully down the drive.

Mary gave a small snort. "Let me guess...you were baking when you came up with it?"

"Maybe," Martha said, laughing. She turned onto the road. "The nursing home is north of town. I'll head that way while you pull up the map."

"Here it is." Mary started the navigation and then laid the phone on the dash where Martha could see it. Her gaze fell to a paper she'd pulled out of Martha's purse when she was digging for the phone. She held it up by the corner. "Hey, what's this?"

Martha gave it a glance. "That's my list of questions for Frank."

Mary eyed the list critically. "Only three?"

"That's all Elizabeth and I could come up with. We were hoping you could add a few more."

She thought a moment and then tapped the paper. "Well, I'd like to know why they didn't keep in touch. Was it just that their lives took different turns, or something else?"

Martha's brows rose, and she tapped her temple and smiled approvingly. "That's using your head. What else?"

"Maybe we could ask if Uncle Paul ever tried to reach out to him after they lost touch."

"Wouldn't hurt." Martha pointed to her purse. "There's a pen in there if you want to write those things down."

"Okay." Mary added her questions to the list and then slid it back inside Martha's purse. When she looked up, they were turning off the main street and heading north out of town. "How much farther?"

"Just a few minutes." Martha tapped the steering wheel nervously, a sure sign that she was thinking of asking something but unsure how to say it.

"Something on your mind?"

Martha looked at her sidelong. "Rafe Porter."

Mary stiffened and turned her gaze to the road. "What about him?"

"Lizzie said she saw you talking to him at the store."

"Just talking," Mary said firmly.

"Okay."

Surprised, Mary watched her sister out of the corner of her eye. It wasn't that she didn't want to open up to her sisters, but Rafe was definitely a subject she wasn't comfortable discussing. Still, she'd expected more of a dispute from Martha and was surprised when she didn't get it.

The navigation system droned directions, and a short time later, Martha parked in front of a brick, single-story building with long windows running the entire length. Twin white columns marked the entrance, next to which was a sign that read MORNINGSIDE NURSING HOME in curving script.

"This is it," Martha said as she put the car in PARK.

A wide cement sidewalk led them straight to the building and through a set of double doors, where they were immediately greeted by a pleasant-looking fellow with a shock of white hair and wide, black-rimmed glasses. He set his coffee cup down and eyed them both with a smile.

"Good morning. What can I do for you ladies?"

Mary edged closer and rested her arms atop the brick and marble counter. "Good morning. We're here to see Frank Mueller. We understand he's a resident here?"

The man nodded, causing his glasses to slip down his nose. He jabbed them back into place with his thumb. "That's right. Is he expecting you?"

"Actually, no," Mary said, "but his wife Selma told us this might be the best time to visit. I'm Mary Baxter, and this is my sister, Martha Watts. Would you let him know that we're here to see him? We're nieces of an old friend of his, Paul Classen."

The man grabbed the telephone, punched in a number, and then went silent while he waited for Frank to pick up. After he explained why he was calling, he replaced the phone and gave them a nod, which made his glasses slip again.

"All right, Frank will see you. I'll have to buzz you into the hall, but then you'll take a left, go all the way to the end, and his will be the last room on your right."

Mary thanked him and followed as Martha led the way. As the man had said, Frank's room was the last one. The door already stood open when they reached it, and Frank Mueller waved to them from a recliner situated near the window.

"Come on in." He pointed to an oxygen tank next to the chair. "Sorry, I can't get up."

Mary blinked, trying hard to hide the surprise she felt from showing on her face. Frank looked twice as old as his pretty wife, and nearly twice as frail, and it wasn't just the oxygen. His shoulders were bent beneath his dark gray sweater, and his face looked pale and haggard, but he smiled at them as they entered, and motioned for them to draw near.

"Well, well, Paul Classen's nieces. Imagine that." He stuck out a gnarled hand, which Martha shook first, and then Mary. "It's a pleasure to meet you both. Please, have a seat."

The room was set up with a bed opposite a small sitting area and a kitchenette. Mary and Martha sat on a love seat covered in navy fabric, which was only just wide enough for the two of them, and then Martha began the introductions.

Frank scratched his temple. "Watts, eh? Any relation to Chuck Watts?"

"He was my husband," Martha said, her face beaming. "Did you know him?"

"I knew *of* him, mostly," Frank said. "He was quite a bit younger than me, but he was pretty good at football."

Martha nodded. "Yes, he played in high school."

"Never went on to play in college? Sure seemed like he was good enough."

"I thought so too," she said, "but no, he never played in college."

Frank's attention turned to Mary. "You certainly look like a Classen girl. Got the same hair and eyes."

Mary smiled. Frank wasn't the first to tell her that she looked like her sisters. "I'm Mary Baxter. I'm the youngest of the Classen sisters."

"I remember seeing pictures of your sisters, but your face escapes me."

"No," Mary said. "Uncle Paul wouldn't have had any pictures of me. He passed away before I was born."

Frank's face suddenly became solemn. "Ah yes. I was very sad to hear that he'd died in a car accident."

"Your wife told us you two were pretty close once," Mary said quietly.

Frank nodded. "Yes, that's true."

"Would you mind telling us how you met?"

"We actually went to school together." Frank chuckled. "But it wasn't anything like the schools nowadays. He and I both went to the old Weavertown school. You ever heard of it?"

Mary shook her head, but Martha rubbed her chin. "You don't mean that one-room schoolhouse out on the Old Philadelphia Pike?"

Frank hooted and scrubbed his knuckles over his balding head. "That's the one. A lot of kids went to school there when I was growing up, but that was long before your time. Anyway, me and your uncle Paul were a year apart in age, but Paul was a tall kid, so everyone always thought he was older. He and I got to be good friends."

"And you stayed close all the way through high school?" Mary asked.

"We sure did. Well, to be more accurate, until I graduated." Frank took a couple of heavy breaths and adjusted the plastic tubing from his oxygen tank. "Sorry. Ever since my heart attack, I get winded pretty easily. My physical therapist has been helping me get my strength back, but I'm still a long way from going home."

"Take your time," Martha urged gently.

He took a deep breath and settled back into his chair. "Anyway, we stayed in touch for a few months after I graduated. I used to get cards and notes from him, but then Paul kind of disappeared for a while."

"What do you mean?" Mary leaned closer, intrigued.

"Oh, nothing mysterious. I just mean that he left Bird-in-Hand. When he came back several years later, I heard he was pursuing some kind of career in art and antiques."

A frown pulled at Martha's lips. "You mean like an art dealer?"

"No, not like that." Frank's eyes scrunched as he thought. "What's the name of that show on TV nowadays...the one about the two guys that travel all over America picking up old junk and reselling it in their shop. You know which one I mean?"

"I have no idea—" Martha began.

"American Pickers!" Mary interrupted. Though she wasn't a huge fan of television, she had seen the ads for this show in particular.

Frank snapped his fingers. "Yeah, that's the one. I watch it every week. I like that short, dark-headed guy. He's a hoot, but he's got a keen eye for antiques." He cocked his head and peered at them. "I heard Paul was doing something like that."

Mary looked at Martha. "Wouldn't that be similar to the store Mama and Daddy were running? Everything they sold was secondhand. Why do you suppose he didn't just go into business with them?"

Martha shrugged and then turned back to Frank. "What else can you tell us about him?"

Frank's gaze bounced between them as they spoke. He clasped his hands over his middle and began twiddling his thumbs. "Uh, not much, I'm afraid. The cards and letters just stopped coming, and we lost touch. I didn't think too much of it at the time. Selma and I were starting our lives together, and then the children came along. We got busy keeping up with them and everything they had going on at school. I assumed the same thing happened with Paul."

"Hmm." Mary tilted her head, thinking. There was no doubt that Frank was ailing, but his mind appeared as sharp as ever. Or was it? Selma said Frank had missed a lot of their kids' "firsts," but here he was claiming he'd been too busy wrapped up in their schedule to keep in touch with an old friend.

She formed her next question carefully. "I don't know if you were aware of this, but there seemed to be some kind of disagreement between Uncle Paul and the rest of the family—bad enough to cause a pretty wide split. Did he ever tell you what it was?"

"A disagreement?" Lines of confusion crisscrossed his face. "I don't understand. Paul's family was always very close. He used to tell me about the get-togethers with all of the aunts and uncles and cousins out at the Classen farm." His cheeks flushed with color. "I never had any brothers or sisters. I used to be a little jealous of his stories."

"So then, everything was fine up to the time he left?"

"As far as I know." He squirmed uncomfortably, his gnarled fingers gripping the arms of his chair. "Hmm. You don't think I had anything to do with the split between him and his family, do you? Paul and I were friends in school, but I have no idea what he got himself into after that."

"Oh, no, it's not that at all," Mary assured him quickly. "We're just trying to figure out what happened because... well... because we know he was buried separately from the rest of the family. It made us think that something must have happened to alienate him from the family."

This time, he looked genuinely confused as he scratched his chin and wagged his head from side to side. "That doesn't make any sense. What could a man do to make his family that mad at him?"

"That's what we were hoping you could tell us," Martha said. "Do you happen to remember the last time you spoke to him?"

Frank squinted, and a grin spread gradually across his lips. "Let's see…yes, as a matter of fact, I do remember."

The concentration cleared from his face as he looked Martha and Mary in the eyes. "It was when Paul brought me the teapot."

CHAPTER NINETEEN

Mary stared, unblinking, while Frank's head bobbed. At long last, he snorted and rubbed one gnarled hand over the other, again and again, the rasping of his skin the only sound in the room.

"Yep, that was the last time I spoke to him. I thought about calling him a couple of times, but then I heard he passed away. I remember thinking what a shame it was that he'd died so young."

"Wait." Mary put up her hand. "Would you mind telling us more about the teapot? He *gave* it to you?"

Frank's eyes rounded at her abrupt tone. "That's right."

"Show him the picture, Mary," Martha urged, motioning rapidly. "You took one with your phone."

"Oh yes." Mary scrambled to yank her phone from her purse and then was all thumbs as she fumbled to pull up the picture. "Here it is," she said at last.

She enlarged the photo and then turned the phone toward Frank. "Is this the teapot that Uncle Paul left with you?"

Frank looked at the phone, tilting his head and swiveling it side to side, squinting as he tried to see. He patted his shirt pockets, felt around the cushions of his recliner, and then finally gave up with a sigh. "Well, rats. What did I do with my glasses?"

Mary and Martha aided in the search, which was quite an endeavor considering the number of half-empty snack bags, tissue boxes, and magazines cluttering the table next to his chair. Finally, Martha located them underneath a stack of newspapers.

She held them up. "Are these your glasses?"

"Ah yes. Thank you." Frank slid the glasses over his nose and reached for Mary's phone. "Now, let's have a look at that photo."

After a moment, he gave a low grunt. "That's the teapot, all right." His finger shook as he pointed. "It really is a thing of beauty. I still remember Paul bringing it by. It was such a surprise seeing him again, after all that time."

"Do you have any idea where he got it?" Mary asked.

"He didn't say." His eyes narrowed as he looked up at her. "That thing has been in my attic for years. How did you get a picture of it?"

"Uh…" Mary looked to Martha desperately for help. They hadn't talked about what they would say if he asked how they'd gotten the teapot.

Martha rose up in her seat and squared her shoulders. "Your wife sold it recently along with a few other things. A friend of ours bought it and brought it to our store to sell on consignment. Mary liked it so much she ended up buying it herself."

Mary blew out a breath. Truth was always the best option, a lesson she and her sisters had learned from their parents. Thank goodness Martha remembered and put it into practice.

Frank gripped the arms of his recliner tightly, making the age spots that dotted the back of his hands pop against his pale skin. "Selma sold the teapot?" A look of panic crossed his face, and he fidgeted nervously. "What about the other stuff?"

"*Other* stuff?" Mary shook her head. "What stuff do you mean?"

"The gold pocket watch and the—" He rubbed his fingers together rapidly and then tugged at the end of his sleeves. "Oh, what do you call them? Those button things?"

"Cufflinks?" Martha offered.

"That's it. The diamond cufflinks. Did she sell those?"

"I'm afraid we don't know anything about those things," Mary said and then frowned. "But you're saying that Uncle Paul brought several items to you and not just the teapot?"

Frank nodded vigorously. "He did. Asked me to hold on to them for him until he could pick them up. I promised him I'd keep them safe. I gave him my word. And I never told Selma about seeing him. I didn't tell anyone."

His words came more rapidly, and his hands fluttered toward the valve on his oxygen tank. "There was something he said he was going to bring to me but he didn't...what was that? Oh, I can't remember—"

"It's all right, Mr. Mueller," Martha said soothingly. "We know you did the best you could to keep your promise."

His fingers still drummed in agitation, but he thanked her with a look.

"How long after the two of you lost touch did he come to you?" Mary asked.

Frank scratched his chin. "Now, that's a little tricky. It was probably eight or nine years or more."

"Did he say why he brought the items to you?" Martha asked.

He shrugged and then relaxed against the back of his chair. "The only thing he would say was that he needed to store them with someone he could trust. Made me promise not to tell anyone. I thought maybe it had something to do with a girl, but he didn't offer to tell me more, and I didn't ask. It had been a long time since I'd seen Paul, but old friends are like that, you know? There are just some people you can always turn to, no matter how long it's been."

His gaze clouded, and sadness crept over his face. "A few months later, I heard Paul had been killed. I kept meaning to pull the things out of the attic and return them to his family, but it never seemed like the right time. After a while..." He held out his hands, palms up. "I forgot all about it."

His face reddened as he looked from Martha to Mary. "You understand, right? I mean, who doesn't have stuff in their attic that they don't ever think about?"

"We understand," Mary said. "It was a long time ago."

He tipped his head, and his lips lifted slightly as if in recognition of the number of years that had passed.

Desperate for something that would help them find Della, Mary leaned forward and clasped her hands. "Mr. Mueller, is there anything else you can remember about the teapot? Anything at all?"

He thought for a moment, his bony fingers scratching lightly over his chin. "I'm sorry, I can't say I do. Paul was in such a hurry when he left it, we really didn't have much time to talk." He sighed and ran his hand wearily over his face. "Anyway, at least the teapot made its way back to Paul's family."

Mary sensed he was getting tired. She glanced at Martha. Reading the unspoken question in Mary's eyes, she reached for her purse and stood.

"Well, I suppose we've taken up enough of your time. Thank you so much for agreeing to meet with us."

"It was a pleasure meeting you," Mary added. Too late, she remembered the list of questions in Martha's purse. Oh well. They'd learned far more than they thought they would.

They shook Frank's hand and then turned for the door. He stopped them when they reached it.

"Look, just one more thing…" He fumbled for a moment and then seemed to find the words. He lifted his chin and looked them squarely in the eyes. "I have no idea what happened between him and the rest of the Classen clan, but the Paul I knew was a good man and an even better friend. For his sake, I hate that things ended up the way they did, but I'm glad…"

Here, his words seemed to choke him. He wiped his hand across his face and then tightened his jaw. "Anyway, it's good to see some members of his family searching for the truth."

The last part raised Mary's eyebrows. She glanced at Martha silently, then turned back to Frank. "Thank you, Mr. Mueller. Goodbye."

They stepped into the hall, and Martha closed the door quietly behind them.

"What did you make of that?" Mary asked when they got back to the car.

"I'm not sure." Martha unlocked the doors, and the two of them climbed inside. "I thought it was going well, until the end."

"I almost felt like he was chastising us," Mary said.

"I thought so too, but why would he do that, unless there was more he didn't tell us?"

"Maybe." Mary frowned as she buckled her seat belt. "Anyway, I suppose we had best get back to the store. Elizabeth is undoubtedly going crazy wondering what we've found out."

"You're probably right." Martha rolled the engine, and within minutes they were headed back through town toward home.

While they drove, Mary gnawed her lip, thinking over everything Frank had said and comparing it to Selma's account. It wasn't that their stories were in opposition...just that there was something odd that she couldn't quite put her finger on.

She sighed and turned her gaze out the window toward the rolling countryside, but it was the front end of a blue car reflected in her mirror that caught her attention and not the acres of green hills.

Mary watched for a while, and then turned to her sister. "Martha, have you noticed that car behind us?"

"What car?" Martha glanced in the rearview mirror and then back at the road. "What about it?"

"Any idea how long it's been following us?"

"No." Martha glanced at it again. "Why?"

Mary looked out her window at the mirror once more. "It's just that it's been right behind us the last two turns."

Martha waved her hand. "Oh, I'm sure it's a coincidence. After all, there's lots of traffic on this road."

"Maybe." Mary rested her arm on the door but kept her gaze pinned to the vehicle behind them. Unfortunately, the car kept its distance so, hard as she tried, she could not make out the features of the driver.

"Martha, would you mind slowing down a bit?" Mary asked.

Martha gave a sigh but complied. The car behind them also slowed.

Mary motioned to a street several blocks ahead. "Turn on Second Street."

"Why?"

"Humor me," Mary said.

Martha turned. Mary held her breath while she waited. Several seconds later, the car behind them also turned.

Mary's heart raced as she reached out and gripped Martha's arm. "Did you see that?"

Her sister's eyes rounded. "I hate to say it, but I think you're right," she said breathlessly. "I think we're being followed."

CHAPTER TWENTY

Martha's breath squeezed from her lungs. Somehow, she managed to keep the car steady on the road. She checked the mirror and then glanced at Mary. "What should I do?"

"Slow down and let them get close enough for me to see the driver," Mary said, craning her neck to peer over the back seat.

Martha tightened her grip on the steering wheel. "Absolutely not."

"Well then, the other option is a high-speed chase." Mary settled onto the seat and looked at her. "How good are your driving skills?"

Martha started to snort in disbelief, until she realized that Mary was teasing. She relaxed her grip on the steering wheel. At the next street, she turned and slowed significantly, letting the car behind them know that they were onto them. To her relief, the driver slowed but spotted them waiting and sped off.

Mary slapped Martha's arm repeatedly in frantic little pats. "Martha, turn around."

"Why would I do that?"

"So we can follow them, of course."

Martha lifted her chin and eased the car up to speed slowly.

Mary twisted in her seat for a glimpse of the strange car. "Martha, they're getting away."

"Exactly, and we're going home safe and sound," she said sternly.

Their gazes collided, and Mary slumped against the seat. "You're right. We should get home. Besides, Elizabeth must be wondering where we are."

In fact, Elizabeth appeared relieved to see them. Sweat dotted her forehead, and her cheeks were flushed as though she'd been hurrying.

"Thank goodness you're back." She wiped her arm over her brow and braced her hands on her hips.

"Lizzie, you'll never believe—" Mary began.

Elizabeth held up her hand. "Not now, Mary. It's been nonstop around here ever since the store opened."

Martha looked around the store. "Why? What's going on? It's not a holiday or anything."

Elizabeth strode to the counter and pulled a newspaper out from alongside the cash register. "I'd say we owe our added business to a little free publicity."

"What?" Martha snatched the paper and snapped it open while Mary read over her shoulder.

"'Painting by Well-known Local Artist Stolen from Family Business,'" Martha read aloud.

Mary snorted and crossed her arms. "Well-known local artist? The only people who know me are the ones who come into our store."

"That's not the part that bothered me," Elizabeth said. Both hands fluttered toward Martha. "Keep reading."

Martha mumbled quietly to herself as she read, and then she stopped dead and stared at Elizabeth. "So much for keeping the family secrets."

"What?" Mary demanded. "What does it say?"

When neither of her sisters answered, she snatched the paper and read for herself. Martha knew instantly when she reached the part that worried her and Elizabeth.

"Oh no," she groaned.

"Yep." Elizabeth took the paper back and folded it in two. "Apparently, some of our neighbors have been talking to reporters."

"Now, now, it's not as bad as all that," Martha soothed.

Elizabeth waved the paper in the air. "I know. I'm just so frustrated, because I think this reporter was trying to make more of this story than there actually is."

She unfolded the paper and read, "'This is the second time in as many months that Secondhand Blessings has been broken into, and not the first time its owners have been embroiled in a garage-sale mystery.'"

She jammed the paper under her arm. "What kind of nonsense is that? Sensationalism, I say."

Their conversation had begun to draw stares. Martha caught Elizabeth's arm and pulled her closer to the door. "All right, let's not work ourselves into a dither. Elizabeth, why don't you go on up to the house and get yourself something to drink? Mary and I can take care of the store this afternoon, can't we, Mary?"

"Of course." Mary took hold of Elizabeth's shoulders and steered her toward the door. "Go on. Get something to eat while you're there. We'll call you if we need anything."

Elizabeth stopped with her hand on the doorknob. "Wait, what about Frank Mueller?"

"Later," Mary said, shooing her out the door.

Once Elizabeth was gone, Mary leaned against it and let out a long breath. "Whew. I'm sorry, Martha. I had no idea my painting was going to create so much trouble." She straightened. "I hope we don't lose customers over this."

"We'll talk about it later," Martha said, passing an apron to Mary and tying another around her own waist. She lowered her head and cast a surreptitious glance around the store.

Catching her meaning, Mary clamped her lips shut and put on her apron. "I'll man the cash register if you wouldn't mind restocking the baked goods table. It looks a little low."

"On it."

Martha moved to the baked goods, and, except for a short lunch break for each of them, the two spent the rest of the afternoon doing little more than waiting on customers. When it was finally time to close, Martha was tired both physically and mentally, since over half of the people who came in had something to say about the missing painting. No one had anything valuable to offer about the theft.

"Well, that was exhausting. No wonder Elizabeth was so frazzled," Mary said as she locked the door.

"Agreed." Martha tossed a towel she'd been using to clean the bakery table into a pile of laundry they would cart up to the house for washing. "And we still have to let Elizabeth know what happened this morning."

"That's true, but let's restock before we head toward the house," Mary said, already reaching for the CLOSED sign. "Otherwise we'll need to do it before we open in the morning, and I for one would like to sleep in."

Martha puffed out a weary sigh. Though her feet screamed for a pair of slippers, Mary was right. *Don't put off until tomorrow what you can do today* was normally something she lived by, but after being chased down the street and then standing on her feet all afternoon, she was seriously considering adopting a new adage.

Once the store was swept and the aisles straightened and restocked, Martha followed Mary up the hill to the house. When they reached the porch, she slapped her hand to her forehead and groaned. "Supper. I meant to get some chicken out of the freezer, but I forgot all about it."

"I'm too tired to eat anyway," Mary said. She tugged on the handle of the screen door. It opened with a screech. "We'll make some sandwiches or something light."

Martha frowned uncertainly. "Are you sure?"

"Positive." Mary took her hand and pulled her inside. "Let's go find Elizabeth. After we tell her what happened today, I'm pretty sure she'll be too distracted to worry about food."

Mary was right. Elizabeth listened, dumbfounded, as Mary and Martha took turns relaying the details of their visit with Frank and all that had transpired after. When they finished, she sank back into her chair, her eyes wide with disbelief. After a moment, her gaze zeroed in on Martha.

"Did you call the police?"

Martha lifted an eyebrow. "And tell them what?"

At her feet, Butterscotch was meowing for attention. Martha gave him a pat on the head and then shooed him into the living room to play with Tink.

"It just seems..." Elizabeth fumbled for words but finally gave up with a sigh. "You're right. It's no crime to follow someone down the street. Still, I'm glad you're both safe." She wagged her finger at them. "You should have told me sooner."

"We did try," Mary said warily, and then laughed. "You were pretty fearsome this afternoon."

"I know, and I'm sorry." She rose from the kitchen table. "But maybe I can make up for it by taking care of dinner."

"Oh, we were thinking sandwiches," Mary said.

Elizabeth held up a loaf of whole-grain bread. "I can do one better."

"Avocados?" Martha asked hopefully.

"Yep, and tomatoes," Elizabeth said.

"Gourmet grilled cheese!" all three said together.

Martha rose and crossed to the refrigerator. "I'll get the blue cheese crumbles."

Mary grabbed a knife. "I'll slice the tomatoes."

The three of them set about making their dinner. While they worked, Martha thought over their conversation with Frank.

"So, did you believe Frank's story about forgetting to return the teapot?" she asked as she carried a pitcher to the sink and filled it with water for lemonade.

Mary laid the sliced tomato on a plate and reached for an avocado. "Of course. Didn't you?"

Martha shrugged. "It's possible that he forgot, I suppose, though I don't understand why he never got in touch with the family after Uncle Paul died."

"Well, that's easy." Elizabeth looked over her shoulder from her spot at the stove and waved the spatula as she talked. "He was probably worried about the timing. After all, he would figure the family was grieving, whether they were or not. I'm sure I would have waited a little while at least."

"And after a few months went by, it's entirely possible that he forgot," Mary added.

Martha grimaced and added the sugar to the lemonade. "I guess so."

"But?" Mary asked after a moment.

"Huh?"

"I felt like there was a 'but' coming."

Martha chuckled. "You know me too well."

She placed the pitcher on the table and watched as Elizabeth laid the slices carefully over the melting cheese.

Mary picked up the plate of tomato and avocado slices and stood next to the stove. "So? What's bugging you?"

Martha turned and leaned against the counter. "It's just that Frank mentioned some diamond cufflinks. The teapot is one thing, but diamonds? Those had to have been expensive. I'm not sure I would have forgotten something like that."

The sandwiches sizzled as Elizabeth added the tomato and another slice of bread, then flipped the whole thing. "Hmm. What else did he say Uncle Paul gave him to hold on to?"

"A gold pocket watch," Martha said. "That could be interesting, if only we knew what it looked like."

Suddenly, the plate that had held the avocado and tomato slices clattered to the floor. Martha jumped, and next to her, Elizabeth pressed her hand over her chest.

"For goodness' sake, Mary," she began, and then stopped as she read the pale shock on Mary's face. She reached out and grasped her arm. "What is it?"

Mary squared her shoulders to look at her sisters. "The thing that Frank said Uncle Paul was going to bring him…Martha, remember, he said something about that?"

Flustered by the intense look in Mary's eyes, she stammered, "W-well, yes, but how does that help us? We don't know what that thing was."

"What if it was a painting?" Mary tossed a pot holder onto the counter and lifted an eyebrow as though waiting for them to make the connection. Finally, she threw her hands into the air. "But what if it wasn't *my* painting the thief wanted? The frame I used for my painting of Uncle Paul, the one that was stolen from the store…I took it from the painting in Uncle Paul's crate!"

CHAPTER TWENTY-ONE

Mary's heart raced. Could it be that the thief who stole her painting wasn't after her painting at all? If the thief *was* after Uncle Paul's painting, then it was doubly likely that whoever broke into Della's apartment was after the teapot as well since it too had belonged to him.

"You think—?" Elizabeth broke off, removed the skillet holding the sandwiches from the hot burner, and set it aside with a clatter. "You think they recognized the frame?" she finished.

"It was very distinctive. I think anybody who knew what they were looking for would probably have recognized it."

All three sisters exchanged somber glances.

"Where's the painting now?" Martha asked. "The one you took from the frame, I mean."

"I still have it. I put it in a box under my bed. I'll go get it."

Her supper forgotten, Mary raced up the stairs. The action caught Tink's attention. She scrambled up the stairs alongside her and then shoved her wet nose against Mary's cheek when she hunched down on the floor.

"Stop, Tink," Mary scolded.

She scrounged under the bed and yanked out the cardboard box. The painting was there, but what about the other things she'd found? She sank onto the floor and wracked her brain. What had she done with the napkin note and map? The last she remembered, she'd stuck them in her jeans pocket. And today was Monday...laundry day.

Leaping to her feet, she yelled, "Elizabeth!"

Wanting to participate, Tink added her own strident barking. Mary ran to the top of the stairs. What was she thinking? They couldn't hear her all the way in the kitchen. She cupped her hands to her mouth and tried again. "Elizabeth, have you done the laundry yet?"

"What?"

Mary shushed Tink and then scooped her into her arms to quiet her barking. "The laundry! Have you done any washing today?"

"Only a couple of loads," she called back. She poked her head into the hall. "I was too tired after leaving the store to really tackle it. Is there something you need? I can throw a load in—"

"No!"

Mary ran back to her room, dropped Tink on the bed, then grabbed the painting before pounding down the stairs where Elizabeth and Martha now waited. Both wore looks of confusion and consternation.

"My goodness, Mary, what in the world is wrong?" Martha asked.

Mary shoved the box at her. "Hold this. I'll be right back. Elizabeth, are all the clothes still in the laundry room?"

"Yes, but why—?"

Mary didn't listen to the rest, but pushed the door to the laundry room open and nearly fell over a basket of neatly

folded towels. That was one load. Elizabeth said she'd managed to do a couple.

She jerked back through the door and skidded to a stop in
the hall. "Where are the jeans?"

"What?"

"My blue jeans. Where are they?"

"In the dryer," Elizabeth said, lifting her hands. "I washed
them along with several other pairs."

"You—oh no." Mary slapped her hand to her head with a
groan. She dashed back into the laundry and yanked open the
dryer door. Several pairs of jeans tumbled out, including the
pair she'd been wearing when she dug through the basement
for Uncle Paul's things. She snatched them up and jammed
her hands into the pockets.

Empty.

She whirled and nearly bumped into Elizabeth, who had
come into the laundry room behind her.

Mary held the jeans high. "Elizabeth, did you take anything out of my pockets before you put these in the wash?"

Normally, Elizabeth would have teased her about emptying
her pockets before dropping her jeans down the laundry chute.
This time, she simply reached for something on the shelf
above the washing machine.

Mary sagged against the dryer with relief when she spied
the napkin and crudely drawn map gripped in Elizabeth's hand.
Thank goodness her sister had adopted their mother's washing
habits.

Elizabeth handed the items to Mary and crossed her arms.
"All right, Mary, what is all this about?"

"Let's go back to the kitchen so we can talk," Mary suggested.

She skirted Elizabeth and led the way back to the kitchen. Martha took the painting out of the box and placed it on the table. Mary set the napkin and map alongside it.

"All right, you remember when I first found this painting, we all thought it odd that Uncle Paul would have it stored in the basement. But then something I remember reading about got me to thinking." Mary pointed to the painting on the table. "What if the person who stole my painting wasn't after my work at all? What if they recognized the frame this painting was in and thought maybe I had simply painted over something much more valuable?"

Martha peered at the painting and frowned. "You're saying this is valuable?"

"Possibly," Mary said. "I think we should check it out."

"But why would someone think you painted over it?" Elizabeth began. "Why would you have done that instead of using a fresh canvas?"

"Money," Mary said. "A lot of artists will paint over old or ugly stuff to save the expense of buying a new canvas."

"Wouldn't that ruin the existing painting?" Martha asked.

Mary shook her head. "Not necessarily. I think whoever took my painting thought that's what happened. They may have intended to try and save the original by removing the new paint and exposing the oil-based painting underneath. It would have meant a lot of work and effort, but if this painting is valuable, it may have been worth it."

"But how will we even know if the painting is valuable?" Elizabeth asked. "We're not art experts."

"No, but I have some friends who might be able to tell us," Mary said. "I can make a few phone calls."

"Do it," Martha said. "Let's see what we can find out."

"Okay," Mary said. "But for right now, I think we need to focus on more pressing questions."

"Which are?" Martha and Elizabeth asked simultaneously.

"Where did Uncle Paul get this painting, and why"—Mary grasped the napkin and the map and held them up together—"did he need these?"

CHAPTER TWENTY-TWO

Mary's hands shook as she slowly lowered the note and the map. If her hunch was right, Uncle Paul was a thief, and the items she'd found buried in the box with his painting were proof.

"Read the note again, Mary," Elizabeth whispered.

Her pale face suggested she had reached the same conclusion, and she didn't like it any more than Mary did.

She bowed her head. "It's pretty simple. All it says is 'Target ready. Don't get caught.'" She held the napkin out and showed them.

Martha wagged her finger toward the napkin. "What about the picture on the front? Where's that place?"

Mary laid the napkin on the table so they could study it together. "Craig's Bistro and Bar." She pinched her lip, thinking. "I've never heard of it."

"Me neither," Martha said.

"Can we google it?" Elizabeth asked.

Mary grabbed her phone and quickly typed in the name.

"That's too broad," Martha said. She motioned toward the phone. "Add something about Pennsylvania."

Mary did and then waited while the results loaded. After several seconds, the only results were for restaurants without

"Craig" in the name. She frowned. "It must have gone out of business."

"Well, I'm not sure it even matters." Martha leaned away from the table and rubbed her eyes wearily. "They may not have even met at that restaurant. It may simply have been the only thing he had handy to write on."

"If he wrote it," Elizabeth said.

"That's true." Mary stared at the bold letters scrawled across the napkin. "We don't even know for certain that this is Uncle Paul's handwriting. I just assumed it was because I found it with his things."

The thought brought a small measure of relief to Mary. She would actually be delighted if her assumptions about Uncle Paul were wrong.

"Do we have anything to compare his handwriting to?" Martha asked. She looked at Mary. "What else did you find down in the basement?"

"It's possible there's something down there," she said. "But I was looking for a frame, so I didn't pay too much attention to the other stuff."

"Let's go look," Elizabeth said. She opened one of the cupboards and took out a flashlight. The button clicked, and the light flickered on. She gave a satisfied nod. "Ready."

Making the trek down to the basement was a lot less worrisome with her sisters joining her. Mary turned on the single light and then led the way to the stack of boxes she knew belonged to Uncle Paul. "Let's see what we can find."

For several minutes, the rustle of cardboard was the only sound as they began to search. Mary found a box stuffed with old clothes and quickly set it aside and reached for another.

"Anything?" she asked as she opened the second box.

"Dishes. Some old cutlery," Martha said, giving a snort of displeasure.

"Just some old books—" Elizabeth broke off and reached slowly into her box.

"What did you find?" Mary leaned close for a glimpse into the box at Elizabeth's feet. "What is that?"

Elizabeth pulled out a large Bible and held it up.

"Is that Uncle Paul's?" Mary asked.

"It has to be." Martha dropped a handful of old spoons back into the box she'd been searching. "Look inside. See if he wrote anything down."

Instead, Elizabeth traced the worn cover with the tip of her finger. The edges were tattered, the spine coming loose from the glue. Even the gilt lettering was faded and almost invisible.

"He read it," she whispered.

"Elizabeth." Martha's voice cracked sharply against the stone walls.

Elizabeth tore her gaze from the Bible to look at her. Martha flicked her fingers toward the pages. "Open it."

Mary laid her arm over Elizabeth's shoulder. Carefully, Elizabeth flipped back the cover, then the first page. Written there was a short inscription: *To Paul, on your birthday. Love, Mom and Dad.*

"Well, we know it was his," Martha said.

"Turn some more pages," Mary said. "Maybe he wrote some notes or something."

Elizabeth turned several pages and stopped. All three sisters leaned in close.

"Bingo," Mary said. On the title page Uncle Paul had written, *Accepted Jesus as my Savior, December 14, 1954,* and then signed his name with a flourish. "Do you think it will be enough to provide us with a comparison?"

Elizabeth hugged it tight. "Let's take it upstairs and check."

Their feet created a shuffling chorus as the three of them hurried upstairs to the kitchen. Elizabeth reopened the Bible to the title page, and Mary laid the napkin alongside it.

"Look at the *a-u*'s." Elizabeth pointed to the letters in *caught* and then the letters in the word *Paul*. "They're the same."

"And he crosses his *t*'s the same way too," Martha added, pointing to the scribbled dash that didn't touch the vertical bar. "Chuck used to do the same thing when he was in a hurry."

Mary's heart sank, and she straightened with a sigh. "Well, I don't think there's any doubt that Uncle Paul wrote this note. The key now is to figure out why."

They were interrupted by the shrill ringing of Mary's cell phone. All three jumped, and Mary hurried to get it.

"Who is it?" Elizabeth asked, her hand pressed to her chest.

Mary shook her head. "Unknown number. Should I let it go to voice mail?"

"Answer it," Martha said. "It may be from the nursing home. Maybe Frank Mueller remembered something."

"Oh, right." Mary swiped her finger across the screen and pressed the phone to her ear. "Hello?"

"Mary?"

Warning shivers ran up Mary's back. She knew this voice.

The line crackled, and then the voice returned. "Mary, are you there? It's Della. I need to speak to you."

CHAPTER TWENTY-THREE

Mary nearly dropped the phone. She fumbled with it, caught it before it clattered to the floor, and then pressed it back to her ear.

Martha's eyes widened as she watched. "Who is it?"

Mary's hand shook as she held up one finger. She turned to the phone. "Della? Is that you?"

Next to her, Martha and Elizabeth gasped and pressed closer.

"Della…Della's calling?" Elizabeth stammered.

"Where is she? Is she all right?" Martha asked.

The questions came simultaneously. Mary waved for her sisters to be quiet. She lowered the phone to the table and punched the Speaker button.

"Della?" she asked again, louder this time. "Where are you? Are you all right?"

"The teapot I sold you—do you still have it?" Della's voice sounded hollow and distant. Worse, it was tinged with panic.

Mary swallowed a knot of apprehension. "The teapot…what? Della, where have you been? We've been so worried."

"Mary, please! Do you still have the teapot?"

Mary looked to her sisters for help. They nodded.

"Yes, I have it," she said slowly.

"What about the other things that belonged to your uncle Paul? Do you still have the painting?"

"What is that painting?" Mary asked. "Della, do you realize your apartment was broken into? The police are looking for you. When are you coming home?"

There was a click, and the phone went silent.

Mary picked it up. "Della, are you still there?"

Nothing. The screen flickered, and then the words "Call Ended" glowed.

"She hung up," Mary said.

"Can you call her back?" Elizabeth asked, gesturing frantically.

"It was an unknown number," Martha said, her shoulders slumping.

"And the quality wasn't good," Mary added. "Like she was someplace with bad reception."

Elizabeth shook her head. "I don't understand. Where is she?"

Mary set the phone down carefully. "She hung up right after I mentioned the police. Why would she do that unless..."

She swallowed hard. Della was her friend. Could she really be on the run from the police? And why? What had she done?

Another thought, this one more sinister, shook Mary to the core. Could it have been Della who followed them home after the visit to the nursing home where Frank Mueller was staying?

Elizabeth touched her arm. "Mary?"

Seeing their concerned stares, Mary shook her head. "Sorry. I was just thinking that we still don't know who broke into the store and took the painting."

"I don't think it was Della," Martha said firmly. She crossed her arms and stuck out her chin.

Mary looked at her in surprise. "Why not?"

"We know Della. It's not like her."

"I don't want to think it's her either, but what choice do we have? She's asking us about it, so obviously she knows Uncle Paul had it. She asked if we 'still' had the painting, which makes me think she knows the wrong picture was taken from the shop."

Elizabeth caught her hand and then took Martha's. "We're all a little upset. Let's take a moment and pray about this before we go any further."

They bowed their heads while Elizabeth led them in a prayer. As she spoke, a bit of the fear and confusion that had been pressing on Mary's heart eased. Elizabeth said "amen," and when Mary looked up, she saw that the lines of tension on Martha's face had also faded.

She gave Elizabeth's fingers a squeeze. "Thank you, Lizzie."

Elizabeth squeezed back and then looked at Martha. "First things first. We need to call John and let him know we've heard from Della. Even if we don't have much information to give him, he needs to know." She reached for her phone. "I'll only be a moment."

She slipped into the hall and spoke in soft tones, then ducked back into the kitchen and held up the phone. "Mary, John would like to see the painting Della was asking about. Would you mind if I text him a picture?"

"Of course not, but you'll need better light." She glanced at the painting and then pushed up from the table and crossed to the wall switches and flipped them all on.

"Do you want me to hold the painting up?" Mary asked.

"That would help." She waited while Mary positioned the painting, then snapped a picture and sent the text. "Done." She pulled out one of the chairs at the table. "Now, where were we?"

The sisters exchanged looks, and Mary's stomach rumbled. She covered her middle with her hand and gave a sheepish grin. "Sorry."

"Our supper." Elizabeth crossed to the stove with a frown. Reaching into the pan, she plucked one of the sandwiches up by the corner. "Anyone for a cold grilled cheese?"

Martha grimaced. "No thanks. I think it'll be cereal for me."

"Me too," Mary said, shooting Elizabeth an apologetic glance. "Maybe the goats would enjoy them."

"I'm sure they would. They'll eat anything." Elizabeth replaced the sandwich in the pan with a sigh and brushed the crumbs from her fingers. "All right, girls, cereal it is. I'll get the bowls."

Martha pulled a box of cornflakes from the cupboard and set it on the counter next to a couple of bananas. "But after this, I say we head for bed and worry about cleaning up the kitchen in the morning. I'm beat."

Me too, Mary thought. "Sounds good to me. I'm more than ready for bed."

She reached for the bananas and sliced them into the three bowls. She truly was tired, but with thoughts of Della and Uncle Paul swirling in her head...

The truth was, it would be a long time before she got any sleep.

CHAPTER TWENTY-FOUR

Martha pushed her pancakes around on her plate the next morning. Next to her Elizabeth did the same, chewing her lip thoughtfully. Across from them, Mary drummed her fingers on the tabletop.

Martha squirmed in her seat. "I have a confession to make."

Instantly, the drumming stopped, and Elizabeth quit biting her lip to look at her.

"I'm wondering if we should have told Della that we still have the teapot," Martha said. "Would it have been better not to let her know that?"

"I don't know," Martha said, "but not telling her would have been lying."

"That's true." Elizabeth sighed heavily. "If only we knew more about it." She peered at Mary. "Maybe we should google it."

"It wouldn't hurt," Mary said. "Who knows what we might find out?"

Martha met Mary's gaze, and in that brief moment, she sensed the depth of concern weighing on her sister's heart.

"Don't worry," Martha said as she pushed to her feet. "Whatever Della has gotten herself into, we'll find a way to help."

"Thanks, Martha," Mary said. She stood and gathered their plates to put them in the sink.

They heard a car pull up in the driveway, and their border collie, Pal, barked a greeting. He waited, tongue lolling, as the sisters came outside to stand on the porch. Martha recognized Bill's truck instantly. He stepped out and lifted his hand in greeting.

"Looks like you have a visitor," Martha said, smiling. She waved back and then turned to Mary. "We have some leftover pancakes if he's hungry."

Mary hesitated before turning for the porch steps. "I'll see if he's busy."

Martha followed Elizabeth back into the house where Tink and Butterscotch greeted them.

"I'll clean up the kitchen if you feed them and the rest of the animals," she said to Elizabeth.

Elizabeth agreed, and a short while later, Mary joined Martha in the kitchen sans Bill. Martha lifted an eyebrow.

"He couldn't stay," Mary said, reaching for an apron. "He said he had a delivery to make."

"And he stopped here on his way?"

Mary shrugged and picked up a dish towel to wipe the dishes Martha had placed in the drainer.

"Everything okay between you two?" Martha asked.

For a long moment, Mary didn't answer. Finally, she set a dry plate on the counter. "Martha, did you lose confidence in yourself after you lost Chuck?"

Martha rinsed another dish and eyed Mary at the same time. "What do you mean by 'lose confidence'?"

"Did you have a hard time making decisions, even simple ones?"

Martha set the plate in the drainer. Mary didn't often trust her with the deep places of her heart. That was a privilege normally reserved for Elizabeth. But in this instance, they had something in common, and she wanted to make sure she took the time to answer truthfully, yet gently.

"Chuck and I used to talk about everything. He was my best friend. Not having him around went deeper than just being lonely. I was bereft." She dried her hands and turned so Mary knew she was giving her her full attention. "For a while, I guess you could say I sort of lost confidence."

A long moment of silence fell between them, during which Mary seemed content to study the cracks in the floor.

"What did you do?" she asked at last.

The vulnerability in her voice pricked Martha's spirit. She should have realized what Mary was going through sooner. Maybe then she wouldn't have waited so long to reach out to her.

She lowered her gaze to her hands, surprised to see that they were shaking. Could she find the strength she needed to share the darkest places in her heart? She begged silently for wisdom as she drew a breath.

"At first, I was angry with God," she began carefully.

Her eyes locked with Mary's, and in their shared grief, Martha found the strength she needed to tell the truth.

"I blamed Him for taking my best friend and leaving me without someone to talk to or lean on. I was hurt and bitter. Worse, I felt alone. Things that I never had to think about—like mowing the lawn or checking a circuit breaker—suddenly those responsibilities fell to me, and I had no idea what I was doing." She chuckled wryly. "The first time I took the car in for new tires, the mechanic asked if I wanted radials or run flats. I told him just to put the same kind of tires on as it had before, because Chuck had picked them out. I still don't know the difference."

She laughed and clasped Mary's hand. "My point is, it took a while, but eventually I realized I still had Someone I could trust. Not only did God want to help me with the tough decisions, He wanted to be there in the everyday tasks. *He* wanted to be my best friend, the Person I talked to and leaned on." She smiled. "And then I moved back home, and God showed me He hadn't left me alone. I have you and Lizzie."

Mary picked up another dish, but instead of drying it, she held it tightly a moment and then set it back down. "You know, ever since Brian left, I've been a little unsure of myself where men are concerned. It's like I'm afraid to trust my own judgment when it comes to discerning the good ones from the bad ones."

"Bill is one of the good ones," Martha said with a wink, "just in case you were wondering."

The surprised look Mary gave her was almost comical.

"What? I'm right, aren't I?" Martha's smile faded. "I would ask you what your heart is telling you, but our hearts are easily fooled. What is the Lord telling you?"

Mary's cheeks flushed. "I haven't asked Him yet."

"Maybe that's the problem," Martha said gently. She laid her hand on Mary's arm. "Trusting in someone other than yourself doesn't have to be a bad thing, so long as the One you're looking to for wisdom is the Lord."

"I'll remember that," Mary said. "Thank you, Martha." She put the stack of dishes in the cupboard. "I'm glad we decided to move back to Bird-in-Hand."

"Me too," Martha said, and deep down, she knew she meant it.

After wiping down the counters and table, Martha followed Mary into the office. Finished with the animals, Elizabeth returned and poured glasses of iced tea, and the three of them gathered around the computer.

"What should we say we're looking for?" Martha asked.

"What if we typed in 'vintage teapots'?" Elizabeth suggested.

"Too broad." Still, Mary typed it in just to show her sisters what she meant. Seeing the number of hits the search generated, both leaned away from the computer in dismay.

"So how do we narrow the search?" Martha asked.

Mary thought for a second and then typed in "vintage teapot with a Janus maker's mark." She went immediately to images, and though there were many teapots similar to the one she had purchased, none matched exactly. After several seconds of scrolling, she sighed and scratched her head.

"Either of you have any ideas?"

Elizabeth grimaced. "You're the computer whiz."

Mary snorted. "Humph. I'm hardly a whiz."

Martha pointed to the word *Janus*. "How did you know what that is?"

Mary's gaze bounced between her sisters. "I had to pick up a few tidbits hanging around with you two."

They laughed, and Mary shut down the computer. "Well, it was worth a shot. Unfortunately, we're going to have to know a little more about our teapot before we can know any more about our teapot."

Elizabeth chuckled as she shuffled back toward the kitchen. "Speaking of tea, who wants more?"

Behind them, Martha smiled. It was good to be home.

CHAPTER TWENTY-FIVE

Mary reached for a stack of copper pie tins that were tilting precariously toward the floor and caught them before they clattered into a heap. That was twice today that someone had nearly knocked them over. She would have to find a better place for them if she didn't want to spend the rest of the afternoon juggling pie plates.

She scooped them up and carried them to the shelves behind Martha's baked goods table. "Hey, do you think you could find room for these? They keep getting knocked over on the main aisle. Besides, I thought they might sell better over here with your stuff."

Martha pointed toward a box on the floor. "Just put them there for now. I'll find a place for them."

Mary started toward the box but only made it a couple of steps before one of the pie plates skewed to the left. Juggling only made the rest of the stack unstable.

She froze in panic. "Oh no—"

She got no further. A hand shot out from nowhere, rescuing the stack and sparing her from embarrassment.

"Whoa there. That was close."

Mary released the air in her lungs in a relieved whoosh. "Wow, thank you. That could have been a disas...ter."

Realizing that her rescuer was Rafe Porter, she fumbled to a stop and stuck out her hand. "I'll take those pie plates."

He rolled his shoulder and grinned. "No problem. Just show me where you want them."

Did over his head count?

Stop it, Mary. He's being nice.

She swallowed a knot of displeasure and pointed. "That box is fine."

"Okay." He strolled—for that was the only way to describe his confident gait—to the box and set the pie plates carefully inside. "There you go."

"Thank you." She grimaced and made herself continue. "That was very nice of you."

He shrugged. "Anything else you need a hand with?"

Mary shook her head and moved away. "No, thank you."

To her dismay, Rafe followed. "Any word from the police on your painting?"

She froze. "What?"

He pointed to the bare spot where the painting had hung. "Your painting. It's such a shame what happened."

Not something she wanted to talk about with him. "I'll have to paint something else to replace it," she said.

His smile widened. "Let me know if you need my help." He made a swiping motion with his hand. "You know...if you need someone to scare you at just the right time and angle."

"I'll do that." She chuckled nervously and wiped her hands down her pants. "So, um, are you looking for something in particular?"

He turned his head and shrugged. "Not really. Just looking."

"All right then." Spying her Amish friend Rachel Fischer near the dishes, Mary raised her hand in a little wave. "Well, I've got customers to care for. Thanks again for your help."

He gave her a quizzical smile and waved back.

Mary felt like she'd been rescued from something. She hurried over to Rachel and angled herself so she stood half-hidden by Rachel's tall, thin frame. "Good morning, Rachel. Something I can help you find?"

Rachel set the platter she'd been examining down. The Amish didn't wear makeup, but she didn't need it. With her glowing skin and bright smile, she was lovelier than some women who spent hours in front of the mirror. She shook her head and tucked a wisp of chocolate-colored hair back into her prayer *kapp*. "Just browsing. The store is busy today."

"Uh-huh."

Her eyebrows rose. "That is *goot, ja?*"

Mary heaved a sigh. "Normally, I would say yes, but today, I'm a little too preoccupied thinking about something else."

Concern lined Rachel's face. "Oh? Is something wrong?"

Mary shook her head. "It's nothing. Sorry. I didn't mean to burden you."

The bell above the door chimed, and Nancy, Beverly, and Linda walked in with their boxes of weekly consignments.

Mary puffed out a breath. "Oops. I forgot last week they told me they'd be coming today. I better go help them." She glanced at Rachel. "Let me know if you need anything."

Rachel touched her arm. "Mary, wait." She tipped her head toward the door. "Aren't they missing someone? There are usually four of them that come in on Mondays, *ja?*"

Mary hesitated. "Yes, normally there are four of them, but Della has been missing for over a week. At least, that's what we thought."

Rachel's eyes widened. "What? Why have I not heard of this?"

Briefly, Mary explained what had been going on, and her suspicions regarding Della's ties to her teapot.

"Unfortunately, we haven't been able to learn much about the teapot, or any of Uncle Paul's things," she finished. "We did an internet search yesterday, but without any information on where the teapot came from, it was pretty hopeless."

Rachel sucked in her lip, her face scrunched and furrowed as she thought. "Hmm...I wonder..."

"Excuse me?" An elderly woman with thick glasses and a bright smile pointed to the apron around Mary's waist. "Do you work here?"

"Yes, I do." Mary glanced at Rachel. "Excuse me for a moment?"

Rachel waved her away, and Mary turned to the elderly customer. "How can I help you?"

The woman's smile widened. "I was in here several days ago, and I noticed a beautiful painting hanging above the baked goods. But I see that it's gone now. Did you sell it?"

Twice in one morning! Mary shook her head and slid her hands into the pockets of her apron. "I'm sorry, that painting is no longer available."

The woman looked genuinely disappointed. "That's too bad. I really liked it." Her face brightened hopefully. "Do you happen to know where you got it?"

A mixture of pride and discomfort filled Mary's chest. "Actually, I painted it."

"You're an artist?" The woman clapped her hands together in excitement. "How wonderful. You're very talented."

Her words had drawn the attention of nearby customers. Mary squirmed under their curious stares.

"Thank you."

"I don't suppose you work on commission?" The woman tilted her head to peer into Mary's face.

"I'm afraid not," she said quickly. "I'm not a professional artist really. It's more of a hobby."

The woman's shoulders fell, and she squeezed her bulky black purse tightly to her side. "Well, you should give it some consideration. I, for one, would love to see more of your work."

She reached inside her purse and pulled out a card. The front was stamped with a wooden artist's palette and several paintbrushes. "I belong to a local artists' group. We meet once a month to share tips and swap stories." She laughed lightly. "It's mostly social, but I do enjoy getting to know some of the local talent. We'd love to have you. Call me if you're interested, and I'll get you the information on the next meeting. My number is on the back."

"I'll do that. Thank you." Mary slid the card into her pocket, proud to know that her painting had been good enough to catch the eye of another local artist.

As the woman walked away, Mary saw another face she recognized. His name popped instantly to mind.

Mary crossed to him. "Jim? Welcome back to Secondhand Blessings."

He inclined his head toward the woman Mary had spoken to. "So, I heard you sold your painting."

Mary frowned. That wasn't what she'd meant to imply. She pasted a smile on her face.

"Can I help you find something?"

He shrugged. "I was interested in the painting, actually. I don't suppose you have any more around?"

"They're along the back wall. Would you like to see?"

He nodded and followed as Mary turned to lead him toward the display. "So you're interested in art?"

He shrugged. "A little, if I see something I really like. I'm looking for something to hang in my apartment back home." He gestured around the shop. "I like your store. You've got a lot of unusual stuff in here."

"Thank you," Mary said. "My sisters and I are very proud of it."

She stopped at the back wall and pointed up to several paintings and pictures tacked at eye level to make viewing them easy for their customers. "See anything you like?"

Jim cupped his chin in his hand and frowned. "These are all very pretty, but I'm more into landscapes. Do you have anything with a country setting?"

"I'm afraid everything we have is right here," Mary said. "But please, take your time looking. I'll come back and check on you in just a minute."

Mary hurried off to meet Nancy, Beverly, and Linda. They waited patiently next to the counter, but today, their bags looked suspiciously light.

As Mary approached, Nancy held hers out with a sigh. "Not much to bring you today, I'm afraid. We've all been so worried about Della that we didn't spend much time at the estate sale today."

Mary took the bag from her gingerly. "Still no word from her, I take it?"

Beverly shook her head vigorously. "We even called the police station to see if they had any new leads."

"What did they say?"

"They said they'll let us know as soon as something turns up." Beverly snorted. "I know they're busy, but I think someone should go down to that station and start a little fire under someone's caboose."

"Now, Beverly," Linda chided. "You know they're doing all they can."

"Yeah, I know." She frowned. "I'm just worried, that's all."

"We all are," Nancy said. She turned an apologetic glance to Mary. "Sorry about this."

"No problem," Mary said swiftly. "Let's get these things recorded for you, hmm?"

With so few items to tally, Mary finished quickly and sent the ladies on their way. Before returning to her customers, however, she placed a call to John Marks. She got his voice mail, left a message asking him to call if he learned anything new about Della, and then slid her phone back into her pocket and went in search of Rachel.

She found her browsing several bolts of cloth. "There you are. Sorry about that. I got a little distracted."

Rachel grasped Mary's arm. "Do not worry about that, Mary. I have goot news."

"News?"

Rachel dipped her head to whisper, "I have been thinking. It is a slim chance…but I think I can help you find out about your teapot."

CHAPTER TWENTY-SIX

Mary stared at Rachel, momentarily tongue-tied by her surprising words. "I don't understand. Help, how?"

Rachel pressed her hands to the apron around her waist as her lips spread in a secretive smile. "We Amish do not have the internet like you *Englischers* do, but we have something just as trusted to go to when we need information."

Suddenly, Mary understood. "The Amish grapevine?"

Rachel laughed. "You could call it that, I suppose. The fact is, many of our members have been around a long time, and they have very goot memories. If you would like, I can ask if any of them remember anything about your uncle Paul and his teapot."

"Would you?" Mary grabbed her hand. "Oh, Rachel, that would be so helpful."

Rachel paused. "But perhaps I should see it before I begin asking questions." She grinned.

"Of course."

Mary looked around, spied Martha, and hurried to tell her where she was going. On her way back to fetch Rachel, a woman with perfectly coiffed blond hair stepped into the aisle. Mary did a double take then shook her head ruefully. The woman was not who she had thought. For just a moment, she'd thought it was Selma Mueller. Though she bore a striking resemblance, this woman was taller and younger.

Still...

Mary stared, openmouthed, as it suddenly struck her why Selma Mueller had looked so familiar the first time they met. Had she seen her in the store? Mary had glimpsed another blond woman who had the build and coloring of Selma browsing the aisles. If it was her, why hadn't she said something when they went to talk to her about the teapot? Could it be she had lied when she said she knew nothing of the teapot's history? What if she had come looking for it, only to discover that Della had already sold it to someone else?

Mary thought back to the conversation with Selma. They had told her Della's apartment was broken into, but they hadn't mentioned her disappearance. If the teapot was valuable...

She swallowed hard. To what lengths would someone go to get it back? But why wouldn't Selma have just asked for it? Mary wracked her brain for an answer.

"Mary?" Rachel looked at her with concern. "Are you all right?"

"Yes, I'm—" She cast one last glance at the woman whom she'd thought was Selma Mueller. If she'd been momentarily fooled this time, she had no way of knowing if she'd really seen Selma in the shop last week. They had scores of customers every day, and many of them were older blond women. "Sorry, I got distracted for a minute. I'm fine. Shall we head up to the house?"

A bit of the concern cleared from Rachel's face, but her smile was still uncertain. "If you would rather wait for another time, I could come back."

"I wouldn't want to make you go out of your way. It'll only take a moment." She gestured toward the door. "Ready?"

Rachel nodded with a little more confidence than before. As they started up the hill, she said, "So tell me about your painting. I didn't see it in the store, so you sold it? That is very goot news, ain't so?"

"Unfortunately, no," Mary said. "I didn't sell it. It was stolen."

Rachel skidded to a stop halfway up the hill to the house. "What? Mary, when did this happen?"

"Last week. Someone broke into the store."

"Oh no! Was anyone hurt?"

"No," Mary said quickly. "We didn't even realize it had happened until the next day."

"Thank *Gott*." Rachel frowned. "Was anything else taken?"

"Oddly enough, no." Mary resumed walking and Rachel with her.

Rachel grabbed the strings of her prayer kapp to keep them from blowing into her face. "I wonder why Martha did not say anything."

"Don't feel bad. I'm sure she would have told you, but we've just been so wrapped up trying to figure things out. She also might have assumed you already knew. It was in the *LNP*."

"Oh, that explains why we didn't know," Rachel said. "We don't subscribe to the Lancaster newspaper."

When they got to the house, Tink and Butterscotch welcomed them. Rachel paused to pat them both on the head and then followed as Mary led her to the china cabinet where she'd placed the teapot.

Mary opened the door and took it out. A look of surprise flashed across Rachel's face.

Her head swiveled toward the tall windows. "You keep it out where anyone can see?"

Mary's grip on the teapot tightened. "I...hadn't thought about it. I suppose I could put it in the safe, at least until we figure out whether or not it is valuable."

Rachel nodded. "I think that might be wise, considering the store was recently broken into." She took the teapot and examined the top and sides, then turned it over carefully to look at the bottom. Her finger traced the image imprinted there. "This is unusual."

"It's called a maker's mark," Mary explained. "I thought maybe it would help us pinpoint where the teapot originated from, but I was wrong."

"A *maker's* mark?"

"Uh-huh." Realizing the Amish likely did not stamp their homemade wares this way, Mary explained the purpose of the mark and what it signified. "This one is a Janus double head," she finished. "It's pretty, but not all that unusual, so we weren't able to glean much information from the mark alone."

Rachel handed the teapot back carefully. "Well, something like that would certainly be remembered. I will mention it when I ask around."

"Thank you, Rachel. Will you excuse me for a moment?" Mary carried the teapot to the office and placed it inside the safe before returning to the dining room. "Okay, it's done. I should have thought of putting it away earlier. I'm glad you suggested it."

"You are welcome, Mary."

Mary turned for the door, but remembering her suspicions regarding Selma earlier, she hesitated.

"Rachel, do you have a minute?"

"Of course," Rachel said, returning. She waited patiently, her hands clasped.

"The woman who sold the teapot in a garage sale is Selma Mueller. Do you know her? Her husband's name is Frank."

"Selma and Frank Mueller," she repeated slowly. *"Ne,* I do not think I know this family. They live in Bird-in-Hand?"

Mary nodded. "Della bought the teapot from them. They claim to be old friends of Uncle Paul's. Maybe you could ask about them when you're inquiring about the teapot?"

"If you would like." Rachel's face scrunched with curiosity. "Is something wrong?"

"I'm not sure," Mary replied. "It's just a gut feeling really, but I'd like to know more about them if I could."

Rachel smiled. "I will ask. If they have lived here long, I am sure someone will know of them."

"Thank you, Rachel."

Rachel walked with Mary to the door, but instead of returning to the store, she crossed down the hill to the spot where her horse and buggy waited. She climbed inside and turned the buggy around before urging the horse down the driveway.

Mary continued down the hill to the store. It had cleared out some since she'd left—or maybe not. She dodged a group of women chatting excitedly about some garden fixtures and made her way past the long line at the cash register to relieve Elizabeth. Anyway, Rafe was gone, so that fact alone gave her much-needed room to breathe.

Mary spent most of the next hour thinking of nothing except cashing out customers. But as the number of people inside the store dwindled, she found herself thinking more and more about the Muellers. Was it really plausible that Frank had simply forgotten about the teapot in his attic for all those years? And they had been followed after leaving the nursing home where Frank was living. Who else would have known they were there? Selma had only given them a vague time frame for visiting, but Frank...

Mary grimaced, trying to recall the details of their visit. The receptionist had called him to announce their visit, and in the time it had taken them to reach his room, he could have easily made a call. Frank had also been told who they were, and Mary clearly remembered him greeting them as Paul Classen's nieces. Then again, if he and Selma were in cahoots, she could have warned him to be expecting a visit. He could have had whoever followed them on speed dial.

The thought raised goose bumps on her flesh.

CHAPTER TWENTY-SEVEN

Martha lifted her head as the sound of buggy wheels clattered up their driveway. Mary had told her and Elizabeth about her conversation with Rachel, so she'd been expecting a visit. She was just surprised to see her so soon.

Climbing out of the flower box, Martha dusted her hand against her apron and called into the house.

"Lizzie? Mary? Rachel is here."

Martha stepped over the flat of impatiens she'd been planting and waited while Rachel climbed down from the buggy. Though she was the same age as the Classen sisters, Rachel was spry and lithe. Was it the Amish lifestyle that kept her so fit? Martha might have been tempted toward jealousy if Rachel wasn't such a good friend. She gave her a hug and then stepped back to peer at her questioningly.

"I didn't expect to see you so soon."

"I know. I thought about waiting until tomorrow, but I knew you and your sisters would want to hear what I have discovered."

Martha grasped her arm and walked with her up the steps. "Come inside. I'll get us something to drink. Would you like some lemonade?"

Rachel nodded. "Lemonade would be goot."

Elizabeth and Mary met them in the kitchen. Both seemed as excited as Martha to see Rachel. While Mary peppered her with questions, Martha gathered the glasses and a pitcher of lemonade from the refrigerator and carried them to the table.

"Mary, give her time to catch her breath," Elizabeth scolded gently. She grabbed the glasses and helped Martha pour.

"So I assume you were able to track down some information on Uncle Paul's teapot?" Mary asked, ignoring Elizabeth's urging and settling into a chair next to Rachel. She rested both arms on the table and leaned forward, her features strained and earnest.

"I think so," Rachel said, hesitantly.

Martha handed her a glass, and she took it with a grateful smile.

"Danke."

"So tell us," Mary pressed. "What did you find?"

Elizabeth slid silently into one of the chairs across from Rachel. Martha sat beside her. She was just as curious as Mary about what Rachel had found, but deep inside, she was troubled. What if they uncovered something unsavory in Uncle Paul's past? How would the rest of the family feel having it brought to light? She curled her fingers around her glass and held her breath while she waited for Rachel to respond.

Rachel's face turned solemn as she looked at Mary. "You were right, Mary. Several people I spoke to *did* remember hearing rumors concerning your uncle Paul after he moved back to Bird-in-Hand." She stopped and lifted one hand. "But I should tell you that a couple of them refused to speak of it because they feared it could be considered gossip."

The knot of apprehension in Martha's stomach tightened. The Amish were careful about not spreading rumors, especially hurtful ones. Whatever Rachel had learned was probably not good.

She swallowed, the movement painful in her dry throat. "It's all right, Rachel. Tell us what you've learned."

Rachel drew in a deep breath and blew it out. "Your family has strong Mennonite ties. Because of this, your uncle was well known among the older members of our community. Several people said he was well liked before he left Bird-in-Hand."

"And when he came back?" Martha asked, sensing Rachel had phrased her words carefully to lessen the sting of whatever she would say next.

Lines formed in the delicate gap between Rachel's brows. She lowered her voice and formed her words carefully, the way Martha used to when she was explaining something difficult to her children.

"People said he was very different. My *grossmudder* has known your family a long time. As a *kind*, she used to come to the farm and play with your grossmudder, Lois. She said she remembered when Paul was born, and how he grew up so handsome and headstrong. But she said when he came back he had changed so much she almost didn't recognize him." She waved her hand over her face. "Like many other Englischers, he had grown a beard even though he wasn't married, but it wasn't just his appearance that had changed. He walked different too. His shoulders were stooped."

She hunched her back, probably the way her grandmother had done when she was explaining.

"And my grossmudder said his demeanor was no longer the same. He did not smile so much, and he was always looking over his shoulder."

Her gaze lit on each of them, and she shrugged apologetically.

Martha took a sip from her glass and let the icy lemonade cool the warmth from her cheeks. "Did your grandmother have any idea what caused the change in Uncle Paul?"

Mary's eyebrows rose at the question, and Martha put her hand on her sister's arm.

"It's all right," she said quietly. "We need to know." She looked at Rachel. "Go ahead."

Rachel clasped her hands tightly around her glass. "It is not goot, I am afraid. Grossmudder said there were many rumors that Paul had begun associating with people of questionable character. It is not that we do not believe in forgiveness," she explained carefully, "but the scripture is clear about choosing one's friends wisely. I heard this repeated several times from people who knew something about Paul."

"Do you know any of these people he was spending time with?" Elizabeth asked.

"I am afraid not," Rachel said. "Grossmudder did not know them either—only that they were Englischers with a reputation for causing trouble. Several people warned Paul about hanging around with them, but he would not listen."

"Well, that's unfortunate," Mary said, "but it's not a crime."

"There is more."

Of course there was. The knot in Martha's stomach crept up and landed squarely on her chest.

Rachel's chin lifted, and her lips thinned. She turned to Mary. "You asked about the teapot?"

"Yes?" she said carefully.

Martha reached across the table and claimed Mary's hand on one side and Elizabeth's hand on the other. Together, they waited silently.

"Grossmudder remembered one thing in particular that I thought you should know." Once again, Rachel's gaze touched on each of their faces. After a moment she said, "The truth is, when I mentioned the teapot, my grossmudder said she did remember hearing rumors of Paul getting mixed up in some illegal activities. People became wary of him."

"Wary...as in shunned?" Martha asked.

"Not shunned in the sense that we cut off ties with him," Rachel said.

"Because he wasn't Amish," Elizabeth said.

Rachel nodded in acknowledgment. "But several people refused to do business with him, especially when the news broke about a valuable tea service that had gone missing from one of the wealthy families who lived nearby."

Mary's eyes widened. "My teapot?"

Rachel turned sad eyes to her. "I am sorry, Mary, but my grossmudder said the rumor back then was that the teapot was stolen."

CHAPTER TWENTY-EIGHT

S tolen." Mary mulled the word carefully, hating the bitter taste it left on her tongue. Poor Della. She had no idea what she was getting into when she bought the teapot. "But why?"

"It was not just any teapot," Rachel said. "The one that was reported stolen was worth many thousands of dollars."

Questions popped like popcorn into Mary's head. Was the person who broke into the store after the teapot? And if so, how did they know it was valuable? And what about Frank Mueller? Had he heard the rumors all those years ago? If so, why hadn't he reported anything to the police? There was no doubt in her mind that is what she would have done—what she *would* do once they finished talking with Rachel.

She pushed aside her lemonade and stood along with Rachel and her sisters.

Rachel wrung the edge of her apron, worry making deep furrows on her brow. "I hope I was right to tell you all of this."

Elizabeth circled the table and pulled her into a strong hug. "Of course you were. Thank you, Rachel."

Rachel's shoulders sank, and she gave a relieved sigh. "I will go now so the three of you can talk. I will let you know if I hear anything else that I think will help."

"Thank you." Mary held the door and then leaned against it wearily after Rachel had gone. She sucked in a breath and shared a long look with her sisters. "Well, I guess we know what caused the rift between Uncle Paul and the rest of the family."

"It appears so," Elizabeth said sadly. "No wonder Daddy forbade anyone from talking about it. He may not have been shunned by the church, but to our family, he may well have been."

"They buried him away from the family, refused to talk about him…" Sorrow soaked Mary's heart. "That's about as close to a shunning as I've ever heard of."

Martha crossed her arms over her chest. "What should we do now?"

Mary pushed off the kitchen door and crossed to the table. "I think the first thing we should do is gather everything that belonged to Uncle Paul and show it to the police, including the teapot. Not clothes or personal items, of course. Only those things that we think might help lead them to Della."

"I agree," Elizabeth said quickly. "Plus, if those things were stolen, we should do everything we can to get them back to the rightful owners."

Martha gestured toward the door. "I'll head down to the basement. I think it will be easier if we bring the stuff up here so the police can examine everything together."

"I'll help." Elizabeth grabbed one of the rubber totes Martha used to carry her baked goods to the store and joined her at the door.

Mary glanced at her watch. "Okay, while you two are doing that, I'll call John and ask him to stop by. It's almost six thirty now. Do you think he'll mind? I would hate to interrupt his supper."

Elizabeth shook her head vigorously. "I don't want to put this off."

"Me neither," Martha added.

Mary rubbed her hands together. "All right, then let's get started. I'll get the teapot."

The three separated to their respective tasks. As Martha and Elizabeth headed downstairs, Mary went to the office and took the teapot out of the safe. If Rachel was right, it was part of a valuable tea service. But valuable enough to put Della in danger?

She tipped the teapot up carefully and examined the maker's mark again. Too bad neither of those heads could talk. She sure would have liked knowing what kind of secrets they could tell.

She blew out a sigh and carried the teapot back to the kitchen table, then went in search of her phone. The last place she remembered having it was in the living room, so she went to look. Spying it on the coffee table, she hurried over and placed the call to John. As Elizabeth had predicted, he was not at all bothered by her call and urged her to gather everything Uncle Paul owned so he could take a look. Mary assured him they had already begun the process and then hung up.

"Oh, the painting." Mary scurried upstairs, retrieved Uncle Paul's painting from beneath her bed, then carried it downstairs and laid the box next to the teapot. Such a shame. It really was beautiful. She opened the box and traced the canvas with the tip of her finger, her heart heavy. "What did you do, Uncle Paul?" she whispered. And what effect were his actions of long ago having on Della today?

She snapped a quick picture of the painting with her phone and emailed it to a few artist friends she hoped could tell her more about it before putting it back in the box. Then, drawing a breath, she crossed to the basement door and cupped her hand to her mouth. "How's it going down there?"

"Ugh. So much stuff," Elizabeth called back.

She emerged a short while later, her face smudged and a spiderweb clinging to her hair. Martha appeared behind her, the tote empty except for a few pieces of crystal that Mary didn't recognize.

For Elizabeth's sake, Mary decided to ignore the spiderweb and pointed to the tote. "Is that it?"

"This is the only stuff we didn't recognize as belonging to the family," Martha explained. She set the tote down carefully and shut the basement door. "But there are so many boxes to go through down there. I think we're going to have to get someone to haul all the boxes upstairs and go through them all. Most of it was clothing and dishes...stuff we could probably just get rid of." The doorbell chimed, and Elizabeth hurried to answer. "I'll get it. It's probably John."

John entered, and Mary let Elizabeth explain what Rachel had discovered. While he listened, he shot several quick glances at the teapot.

He touched the lid and met Mary's gaze. "This is the one in the photo you gave me?"

She nodded. "I'm sorry, but we haven't been able to find out much more about it."

He shook his head. "Don't worry. That's our job." His gaze shifted to Elizabeth. "But I may have to take your uncle's things with me to the station while I see what we can find out."

"Of course," she said without hesitation. "We expected as much. Thank you so much for coming down, John."

Martha motioned toward the nearly empty tote. "You can take that with you, if you'd like."

He agreed, and Martha and Elizabeth helped him load the tote with the painting and teapot.

After John left, the sisters went into the kitchen. The anxious feeling clawing inside Mary's stomach made sitting impossible. She paced the floor, recalling everything Rachel had said and wishing she could speak to her father once more so he could unravel this mystery once and for all.

Elizabeth looked every bit as strained and anxious as Mary felt. Her fingers twisted the hem of her blouse, the pale color of which seemed to match her white cheeks.

Martha sank heavily onto a chair at the table and threw her hands into the air in frustration. "This makes no sense. Why would Paul go from being a wonderful, kind man people liked to a thief everyone shunned?"

Elizabeth joined Martha at the table—like a pair of gloomy birds with their downcast looks and sour faces. "And if our family won't or can't tell us what happened, who could?"

Mary drummed her fingers against the counter. "We need to talk to someone who knew him."

"Like who?" Martha's head jerked up. "Aunt Gertrude isn't talking, we can't get ahold of the other aunts or Uncle George, and we've already visited with Frank and Selma Mueller."

Elizabeth snapped her fingers. "What about Duffy Porter? He's lived in Bird-in-Hand forever. Surely he knew Uncle Paul."

Lived in Bird-in-Hand.

Suddenly, words she'd heard uttered at the store flashed into Mary's mind.

"You say you had an uncle named Paul Classen? My grandfather went to school with a man by that name."

"Jim Olson."

Her sisters stopped talking to look at her.

Mary lifted her chin. "Jim Olson," she repeated, louder. "The guy I spoke to in the store the day I bought the teapot from Della."

Mary explained how Rafe had inadvertently let the subject of her painting spill to Della, and how Jim overheard the two of them talking.

"He told me his grandfather had gone to school with Uncle Paul and he gave me—"

She broke off, stunned, and slapped her hand to her forehead.

"Mary? What is it?" Elizabeth stepped closer, her eyes dark and questioning.

Mary turned to her. "His card. I asked if his grandfather would be willing to talk to us, and he said to give him a couple of days, and he would check with him. He gave me his business card with his contact information."

"Do you still have it?" Martha asked sharply.

"Somewhere." Mary fought a moment of panic as she struggled to remember what she'd done with it, then gave an agonized sigh. "It's no good. I put it in my jeans pocket. I'm sure it's gone through the wash by now."

She shot a glance at Elizabeth, who lifted her hands and shrugged. "I'm sorry, Mary. I didn't find it."

"Don't worry about it. It's my fault." She let her shoulders droop and shook her head in exasperation. "How could I have forgotten?"

"It's not all that bad, Mary," Elizabeth said, soothingly. She turned to Martha. "Maybe we can figure out who his grandfather is."

Martha gave a curt nod. "His last name is Olson?"

"That's right." Mary pushed from the counter and joined her sisters at the table. "What are the odds that we'd be lucky enough to find out he had the same last name as his grandfather?"

"Mmm." Martha rubbed her chin thoughtfully. "Olson is a pretty common name in this part of Pennsylvania."

Mary brightened. "I know…we can look in some of Mama and Daddy's old church directories. If Uncle Paul and Jim Olson's grandfather went to school together, he was from this area. There might be a slim chance the two families also attended the same church."

Elizabeth's eyes shone approvingly. "Good thinking, Mary. It's worth a try. I'll get the directories."

She left the kitchen and returned a few minutes later with several old books in her hand. Dividing the stack in three, she passed several books to Mary, some to Martha, and kept some for herself.

Martha flipped open the cover on the first book. "All right, so we're looking for anyone named Olson."

"Specifically, someone who would have been around the same age as Uncle Paul," Elizabeth added.

"You're right, Lizzie." Mary checked the dates on the directories and pushed several of the more recent ones aside. "I guess there's a possibility that Jim's grandfather still goes to the same church and would be in a more recent directory, but I think our best bet is to look for something older than around 1960."

"Like these." Elizabeth held up three of the books from her stack. "Good thing Mama didn't believe in throwing these away. She kept them as a record of the church's membership over the years, but they sure are handy now." She slid two of the books across the table, one to each of her sisters.

Mary opened hers excitedly. Perhaps this was the lead she'd been hoping for...something that would finally give them the information they needed about their uncle Paul.

"Here's one." Martha turned her book and tapped a long column.

These books were thinner than their more recent counterparts, and consisted only of names and addresses. A few also included phone numbers. Fewer still had photos.

"William P. Olsen." Mary shook her head. "No, that's not right. I only glanced at his card, but I'm almost positive Jim Olson spelled his name with an *o-n*." She gave a growl of frustration. "If only I hadn't lost that card."

"Don't worry, Mary. We'll keep looking." Elizabeth's gaze dropped down to her book. "Oh, here's another one. James D. Olson."

Mary reached for Elizabeth's book and turned it to read the address. "No phone number but...Fish Farm Road? That's just the other side of town." She met her sisters' gaze across the pages. "You don't suppose he could still be in the same place?"

"It's worth a try," Elizabeth said. She glanced at Martha hopefully. "Right?"

Martha glanced at her watch. "It's only seven thirty. I suppose we could try—"

"I'll drive." Mary jumped up and snatched her keys off the rack next to the door before Martha could change her mind.

Fortunately, the days stretched longer this time of year. The sun had not quite set by the time they pulled up to the old farmhouse the directory said had once belonged to James Olson. Mary knocked hesitantly on the screen door and then fidgeted on the steps while she waited for someone to answer. Finally, a woman about their age appeared, wearing a flowered apron, her hair dripping from a messy bun at her nape.

"Can I help you?" she asked through the screen.

"Is this the Olson residence?" Mary asked.

The woman put her hand to the latch on the door and eyed her curiously. "Yes."

"My name is Mary Baxter. These are my sisters Elizabeth Classen and Martha Watts."

The woman looked at each of them and then returned her gaze to Elizabeth. "You say your last name is Classen?"

Elizabeth stepped forward. "That's right. My parents were Henry and Elma Classen."

"And our grandparents were Simon and Lois Classen," Martha added. "We think that James Olson may have gone to school with one of our uncles. Does the name Paul Classen sound familiar?"

The woman thought for a minute and then shook her head. "No, I'm sorry, not that I recall." She pushed open the screen and stepped out onto the porch with them. "But are you looking for James Michael Olson, or his father, James David?"

Martha shot a glance at Mary.

"Mostly likely, it's James David we need," she said. She turned to her sisters. "The directory said James D. Olson."

Martha nodded. "That's right."

"Oh, then I'm afraid you're at the wrong place." The woman hitched her thumb over her shoulder. "This is the James Michael residence. James David is my husband's father, and he hasn't lived here for almost ten years."

Mary clasped her hands as a host of possibilities about why that might be rolled through her brain. "Oh?"

Mrs. Olson propped her hands on her hips. "He moved into an assisted living facility after he broke his hip and couldn't get around so good anymore." She eyed them for another second and then seemed to make up her mind. "I can tell you how to get there if you're interested in visiting him."

"Would you?" Mary took out her phone and prepared to type in the address. "That would be so helpful." When she finished typing in the information, she slid her phone back into her pocket. "Thank you so much for your time."

"You're very welcome." A smile peeked from the woman's lips, making her appear friendlier.

"Mrs. Olson, your son wouldn't happen to be visiting by chance, would he?" Mary asked.

The smile faded. "My son?"

Mary nodded. "Yes. I met him at the store my sisters and I run together. He was the one who told me his grandfather had gone to school with our uncle."

Mrs. Olson fumbled for the doorjamb and leaned against it heavily. "You've seen Jimmy? How long ago?"

"Wilma?" a voice called from inside the house.

Mrs. Olson jerked her head toward the sound. "I'm out here." She turned back to Mary. "That's my husband. Please don't mention that you spoke to Jimmy."

By the look on her sisters' faces, they were as shocked by the request as Mary felt. She didn't have long to ponder it, however, before a thickset man with gnarled hands and broad shoulders appeared.

"I'm heading out, Wilma—"

He broke off when he caught sight of them. "Sorry. I didn't know we had visitors."

"These ladies are looking for your daddy, James," Mrs. Olson said, tugging nervously at her apron.

One eyebrow quirked, and he trained his gaze on Mary and her sisters. "You know my father?"

"Our uncle did. He went to school with him," Mary said. "We were hoping to ask him a couple of questions."

At a loss as to what she would say if he asked why, Mary held her breath and waited. Instead, Mr. Olson looked out at the setting sun and grunted.

"Well, I need to get back to that last field before it gets dark. Wilma can answer any questions for you. If you ladies would excuse me?"

Mary blew out the breath as he passed. Not that Mr. Olson had seemed unkind or rude, but his wife's plea when he appeared had certainly made things awkward. They waited while Mr. Olson climbed into a dusty pickup truck before turning back to Mrs. Olson.

"Thank you," she said quietly, her shoulders sagging. "I'm so sorry about all of that. It's just, things are still pretty strained between my husband and our son Jimmy. He left home after his father insisted that he take on more responsibilities on the farm."

"He didn't want to be a farmer?" Elizabeth asked.

"It was one of many things he and his father didn't see eye to eye on. Jimmy loves art. His father views it as a waste of time. Jimmy left Bird-in-Hand determined to prove his father wrong." Mrs. Olson sighed sadly and smoothed the ruffled hem of her apron. "Anyway, it's been almost five years since we've spoken to him, and I didn't want James to be upset. Without Jimmy, he's had to work a lot harder to keep this place going. I've tried to help pick up some of the slack, but there's only so much I can do."

"I'm sorry," Mary said, placing a light touch on Mrs. Olson's arm. "We'll be praying for your family."

Mrs. Olson appeared taken aback by the statement, but she managed a weak smile as she blinked away sudden tears. "Thank you. I appreciate that."

The three said goodbye, and then Mary led them back to the car. By now, the clock on the dash read after eight. Instead of heading to the assisted living facility where James D. Olson now lived, she pointed the car toward home and glanced at Elizabeth in the rearview mirror.

"Probably best if we get some rest and tackle this problem in the morning, don't you think?"

Elizabeth agreed and tapped Martha on the shoulder. "What do you think about helping me at the store tomorrow? Mary can head out early while you and I get things up and running."

"I think that's a good idea," Martha said, then turned to Mary. "But besides going to visit Jim Olson's grandfather, would you mind adding one more stop to your list?"

Mary darted a quick glance at her and then back at the road. "What do you have in mind?"

"Well, Elizabeth mentioned Duffy Porter earlier. I think it would probably be a good idea to visit him too, since we're trying to pinpoint anyone who might have known Uncle Paul. Would you be all right talking to him?"

Mary squeezed the steering wheel. Talking to Duffy was fine, but it almost certainly meant she would also be bumping into Rafe.

"Or we could do it later, if you'd rather," Elizabeth said softly.

Mary gritted her teeth and shook her head. "No, that's all right. I can do it."

Thankfully, they let the subject drop. Soon, Elizabeth settled into the back seat and Martha turned her eyes out the darkened window, leaving Mary to ponder her worrisome thoughts alone.

She thrust out her chin and pressed harder on the accelerator. Being around Rafe made her feel awkward and insecure, two emotions she'd hoped to be rid of the day Brian walked out her door. But no matter how inept she felt where Rafe was concerned, she wasn't about to let anything get in the way of finding out what she could about Della or Uncle Paul. After all, the man was just a visitor to Bird-in-Hand.

As she made the turn toward home, she put action behind her promise to Mrs. Olson and lifted a prayer for her, her husband and son, and for restoration to come to their family. She ended her prayer with a wry smile on her lips. *A little restoration wouldn't hurt our family either.*

CHAPTER TWENTY-NINE

The assisted-living facility in Lancaster that James Olson called home was a stately, colonial-style building with a grand entrance and tall pillars at the center, and two long wings sweeping out from each side. Mary ducked into a parking spot and then made her way toward the entrance through two rows of neatly trimmed boxwoods. A sign on the door said to ring the bell for admittance, so she pushed the button and then stood back to wait. Above the door, a camera lens hummed as it moved to focus on her, and she fought the inclination to reach up and smooth her hair, choosing instead to smile brightly.

"Can I help you?"

The voice crackled from a speaker box mounted on the door frame.

Mary cleared her throat and leaned toward it. "Mary Baxter, here to see James Olson. I believe he's one of your residents?"

"Come on in. Be careful. The door is heavy."

The door buzzed, and Mary reached out to pull hard on the handle. Inside, the lobby was cool and elegantly appointed. Soft instrumental music played over the sound system. Mary recognized it as being one of her favorite hymns. She moved to the reception counter where a young woman wearing navy scrubs beckoned.

She slid a pen into her pocket and smiled. "Hi. Sorry about the door. We're getting it fixed."

"No problem."

The woman pushed a clipboard across the desk to Mary. "You're here to see Mr. Olson? Just sign in please, and take one of the visitor badges." She pointed to a basket on the end of the counter.

Mary signed in and then reached for one of the badges to pin to her shirt. While she fumbled with it, she nodded toward the door. "So, is the buzzer a security measure?"

"Yes," the woman said. "We have two wings here. One is for people requiring minimal care. The other is for patients with dementia or who require extensive, round-the-clock care."

"Ah, I see." Mary finished with her badge and rested her arms on the counter. "So I guess that would help you keep track of everyone who comes and goes."

"That's right." The woman reached under the counter and pulled out a diagram of the facility. She circled one of the numbers, then pointed down a long hall. "Mr. Olson's room is through those doors. Just follow the diagram, and if you get lost, check in with the nurses' station at the end of the hall."

Mary took the diagram and turned for the doors. "Will do. Thank you."

Her footsteps echoed dully in the long corridor. She checked the diagram before turning left, followed quickly by a right. At last, she found herself outside Mr. Olson's door. Her light knock was greeted with a gruff, "Come in."

Mary reached for the knob hesitantly, only to have it yanked from her hand as the door swung inward.

Mary's mouth dropped open. In fact, it was the younger version of Mr. Olson, not the one she'd been expecting, who met her at the door.

Jim's eyes widened at the sight of her. "Mary Classen Baxter. Please, come in."

Mary stepped over the threshold. The room was large and decorated well, if sparingly. A large bed dominated the space, and next to it, an oversized recliner. James Olson didn't occupy either. She turned to look at Jim.

He slid his hands into the pockets of his jeans. "What a nice surprise."

Mary smiled. "It is." She motioned toward the empty room. "I was hoping to speak to your grandfather. You mentioned he might be able to tell me something about my uncle when you were in the store."

The confusion cleared from his face. He pulled his hands from his pockets and ambled toward a small table in the kitchenette area of the apartment. Newspaper clippings were scattered across the top. "Right, right. I forgot all about that." He gathered up the clippings, stuffed them into a cardboard box, and then pushed the box into one of the cupboards. When he finished, he pulled out a chair and indicated it was for her. "Sorry about that. Gramps likes to clip coupons. Please, have a seat."

She did, and he motioned toward the refrigerator. "Can I get you something to drink?"

She declined with a shake of her head. "I'm fine, thank you."

Jim circled the table to sit across from her. "I'm afraid you've missed Gramps. It's time for his dance lesson. He's taken up learning to waltz. Says it helps with his hip." He glanced at a clock above the window. "You're welcome to wait, if you'd like. He should only be another fifteen minutes or so."

She still had plenty of time before she headed out to meet Duffy. "Are you sure? I'm not keeping you from something?"

"Nah." Jim leaned back against his chair. "These visits with Grandpa can be pretty boring sometimes. Mostly he just likes to talk." He pointed to a checkerboard on the counter. "Or beat me at checkers."

Mary laughed. "My grandparents were pretty good at checkers too." She sobered and sat up in her chair. "Listen, I'm sorry I didn't call first. I misplaced the card you gave me."

He waved dismissively. "No problem. After I told him I'd been to the store, Gramps was pretty eager to meet you. I'm sure he'll be glad you stopped by."

The thought pleased Mary, as did the small talk that Jim seemed quite adept at making while they waited for his grand-father to return. He told her that he traveled quite extensively, though when she asked about his line of work, he merely gave a wave of his hand and went on talking about a painting he'd admired the last time he was in Venice.

The door opened, and his grandfather entered, ending their conversation but starting a new one when he learned that Mary was related to Paul Classen. He invited Mary into the small seating area, and then, with the help of his grandson,

James hobbled toward the recliner. His limp was slightly more pronounced when he released Jim's arm and maneuvered around to lower himself into the chair, but he managed it without too much effort. Mary joined Jim on a narrow couch, their knees almost touching, while they waited for James to make himself comfortable.

Once he was settled, his pale blue eyes took on an interested gleam as he studied Mary through his smudged bifocals.

"So, you're one of the Classen girls. I must say, it sure is a pleasure to meet you. I always did like your family. They were some good people, and that's a fact."

"Thank you," Mary said, her cheeks warming. She motioned to Jim. "Your grandson tells me you knew my uncle."

"Oh, I knew several of your uncles." He pointed his knobby finger at her. "Your father was Henry, right?"

"That's right."

He nodded and leaned back to rest his elbows on the arms of the chair. "Yep. I thought so. You look so much like him. That Henry was a character. I used to love to hear him sing. He had a real rich baritone. Boy, that guy could carry a tune, and that's a fact."

Jim caught her gaze and gave an apologetic shrug. "Uh, Grandpa, Mary would like to know what you remember about her uncle Paul."

"Who?" James cupped his hand to his ear.

Jim eased to the edge of the couch and spoke a little louder. "Paul. You remember him? He was Henry's younger brother."

"Oh, Paul." James nodded and dropped his hand. "Yes, I remember him." His gaze sharpened as he looked from Jim to

Mary. "Paul was very different from the rest of the Classen clan. He had a wild streak. Wasn't so proper."

"So I've heard," Mary said.

Jim put his hand on his grandfather's arm. "Gramps, I told Mary you and Paul went to school together. Remember?"

He nodded. "That's right. The old Weavertown school."

His gaze grew misty, and he tipped his head back and launched into a lengthy account of the history of the school, including the many people he knew who'd gone to school there with him.

His gaze sharpened and focused on Mary. "Do you know Andrew Vance? His folks used to own that old farm on Millhouse Road, just past Smith's pond."

Mary shook her head. "No, sorry, I don't."

Ignoring her denial, he began naming all the members of the Vance family, including their numerous children, grandchildren, and cousins. Mary cast a surreptitious glance at her watch. At this rate, she'd never make it to the Porters' house.

Jim seemed aware of her discomfort. He tapped his grand-father's knee and pointed to Mary. "Hey, Gramps, maybe you could tell Mary here a little more about Paul. Didn't he leave town shortly after you graduated?"

Thankful to Jim for directing the conversation, Mary cast a small smile his way.

James scratched his head as though struggling to recall something. "Yes, I remember Paul leaving Bird-in-Hand. It was all he talked about in school. He was going to travel the world, see Paris and Rome. Course, he didn't have the money to do all that. Didn't bother him though. He said he was going work his way across Europe. Of course, all of that changed when—"

Jim tapped his arm again. "Gramps, you went to Europe, didn't you?"

James looked confused a moment, but then his gaze locked with his grandson's, and he nodded. "Yes, that's right. Your grandmother and I took a trip back in '67. We went to Hamburg, where some of her family was from."

Once again, he was rambling. Mary waited for a break in his thoughts. "Mr. Olson, do you remember a Frank Mueller who went to school with you?"

James squinted at her. "Frank Mueller, Frank…Why yes, I do recall a boy by that name. I didn't know him very well, although I remember him being a good friend of your uncle's. Since I was the only boy in my family, I had to help out on our family farm more than Paul did on his, so I missed a lot of their fun."

She really did need to be going. Mary thanked James and Jim for their time and stood.

"This has been wonderful, but I promised my sisters I would make one more stop before I head back to the store." She bent to shake James's hand. "Thank you so much for speaking with me, Mr. Olson."

The old man gripped her hand in both of his and drew her closer. "Your uncle was a good man, Mary Classen. I do hope you know that, despite everything that happened."

She stared at him in bemusement. "What?"

Before he could respond, Jim leaned forward. "She's Mary Baxter, Gramps. Classen was her maiden name." He shook his head at Mary and gestured toward the door. "Sorry about that. Can I walk you out?"

Mary glanced at him and then back at James, who was eyeing her rather sadly. "Oh, but—"

"He gets a little confused when he's tired, right, Gramps?" He clapped his grandfather on the shoulder. "I'll be back in a few, okay? I'm going to walk Mary out, and then I'm going to run to the store. Do you need me to grab anything for you?"

James shook his head, the motion causing his glasses to slip down his nose. He jabbed them back into place with his thumb. "No, that's all right. I have everything I need."

"Okay. Thanks, Gramps."

Jim grabbed a navy-colored sport coat from a row of hooks, then pulled the door wide for Mary to pass through. His meaning clear, Mary reached for her purse. Obviously, Jim was protective of his grandfather, but she dearly wished she could have asked him what he'd meant when he said "despite everything that happened."

As they walked down the hall, Mary turned to Jim. "Thank you so much for letting me chat with your grandfather. He seems like a really interesting man."

Jim hunched his shoulders, his sport coat swinging from the crook of his arm. "Oh, he is that. Grandpa has a lot of stories to tell. I just wish I'd written some of them down...you know...before his facts got so mixed up. It's hard to tell nowadays what's real and what's not."

Mary's steps slowed. "You mean he has dementia?"

"Didn't the nurse tell you?" Jim's shoulder rolled in a shrug. "Yeah, the last few years have been really tough. Gramps is still in the minimal care wing, but they'll probably have to move him over eventually. I probably should have warned you about it when I offered to let you come by to talk to him."

"No, no, that's all right," she said, biting her lip. She hiked her purse strap higher on her shoulder, thanking Jim as he pushed the buzzer then held the door open, leading them outside.

Mary stuck out her hand. "Well, thanks again."

"My pleasure." Jim shook her hand then slid his arms into the sleeves of his sport coat. "And listen, feel free to stop by again." He reached into his pocket and pulled out another card. He held it up, his eyes twinkling. "Don't lose this one."

"I won't." Mary slid the card into her purse then gave one last smile. "Bye, Ji—"

The words froze on Mary's tongue as she stared at Jim. His smile faded, and then his gaze dropped to see what she was looking at.

His sport coat was missing a button.

CHAPTER THIRTY

"Mary, are you all right?"

Jim reached out and touched her arm, his eyes reflecting his confusion. Mary blinked and then managed a small nod.

"Uh, yes. Sorry. I just noticed...you're missing a button."

She pointed to his jacket. Jim grabbed the edge and held it out for inspection. "Oh yeah. I lost it sometime last week."

"I think I may have found it," Mary said, her eyes narrowing as she watched his face for his reaction. "It was on the floor in our store."

"Really?" He shrugged, his smile almost flippant. "Huh. I guess it must have come off when I was in there shopping. I'll have to stop by again and get it from you."

"Oh, I don't think it will be much use. It was broken. I don't think it just fell off."

"Maybe."

His smile persisted, but something about it made it seem artificial.

Mary motioned toward her car. "Well, I'd better get going."

"Okay. See you around, Mary."

He waved, then turned and walked away. Mary watched him go, suspicion flaring like fire inside her head. Why hadn't Jim let his grandfather respond when Mary asked what he'd meant by "everything that happened"? She had assumed he was directing the conversation in an attempt at being helpful, but what if it was something else? What if he had been carefully orchestrating what he wanted her to hear? And did his grandfather even have dementia, as he'd claimed?

Mary headed to her car, but instead of pulling onto the highway, she started the engine and slowly circled the parking lot. She hadn't seen which vehicle Jim climbed into, but there was only one other car exiting the parking lot.

It was blue.

Mary's breath hitched as she recalled the car that followed them home after they left from visiting Frank Mueller. There were thousands of blue cars in her little corner of Pennsylvania. The odds that it was the same one were slim. Still…

As Mary pulled onto the road, something Mrs. Olson said popped into her mind. Jimmy loved art—so much that he'd left his parents and the family farm behind. Yet she was almost certain he'd told her that he was only mildly interested the day he came into the store looking for something to hang in his apartment. Why would he lie?

Mary's heart rate sped as she pondered exactly what Jimmy had said he wanted. Not just any painting…he was looking for a landscape.

One with a country setting.

Like Uncle Paul's painting!

Instead of driving to the Porters', Mary turned her car toward home, anxious to share what she'd discovered with Martha and Elizabeth. Mindful of her speed, Mary forced herself to navigate the roads slowly, in spite of her racing thoughts.

Thunderclouds had begun to gather, casting the day into premature gloom. She flicked on her headlights and turned into the driveway.

The sight that met her made her gasp. A blue car! And leaning against the door was Jim Olson. What was he doing here?

Mary clutched her purse to her chest and exited her car, squinting as he made his way toward her. "Jim?"

His grin widened. "Hi, Mary. I bet you're surprised to see me so soon."

"Uh, that depends." Mary cast a look over his shoulder toward the barn. "Were you coming to get your button?"

He chuckled and shook his head. "Not exactly. I was coming to see you. All that talk about art this morning got me thinking. I really liked the painting you did." He stepped closer. "The one overlooking the cemetery? I was pretty disappointed when I heard it was gone. I was hoping I could talk to you about commissioning another one since, you know, I didn't get the one I was after."

The one he was really *after.*

Mary fought a shudder and backed against her car door as he stepped even closer.

She held up her hand, realized it was shaking, and propped it on her hip. "That's really kind of you, but I'm afraid I don't have time to talk at the moment. Maybe you could stop by later this week?"

His lips thinned as he shuffled from foot to foot. "I'm afraid that won't work. I'll be heading back home in a couple of days. Until then, I'll be busy getting all my grandfather's affairs in order."

He pointed to his temple. "Like I said, Gramps isn't doing so well. Not all there, you know?"

"Yes, you told me." Mary shot another glance toward the barn and wished desperately for a glimpse of her sisters.

Jimmy crossed his arms, stretching the seams of his coat. "It's weird how the mind works, isn't it? Gramps has been forgetting stuff that happened yesterday but dredging up all kinds of things from fifty years ago."

"Really?"

"Uh-huh. It's almost like he's reliving his glory days. He's been telling me all kinds of stories about when he was young, which is why your painting struck such a chord with me, I suppose." He held out one hand in appeal. "Listen, I know you said you haven't got a lot of time, but I really only need a minute." He shot a peek over her shoulder. "Are your sisters working in the store? Do you think they would mind if I came in to talk to you about doing another painting for me?"

By now, he was near enough for Mary to read the earnest lines of his face. Tension tightened the skin around his lips and eyes. He *really* wanted to come in, which meant she needed to think up an excuse, and quick.

She slid around the front end of the car in what she hoped looked like a casual saunter. "Normally, I'm sure they wouldn't mind a bit." She held up her hand when it looked as though he might follow her to the porch. "However, like I told you before, now is not a good time. You see, we're expecting Officer Marks any moment. There have been some new developments regarding the break-in at the store that we need to discuss with him. But I can swing by the assisted living facility tomorrow, if you'd like."

Jim's posture changed. His chin lifted, and he straightened his spine before starting forcefully up the path. He stopped at the porch and put out his hand to grip the railing. "No good. I'm afraid it really has to be today."

"But…" Mary licked her lips nervously. "Officer Marks really will be here soon," she said, her breaths coming faster and making her sound winded.

"Well then, I suppose we'd better hurry."

Mary swallowed hastily and tore her gaze from Jim's face. Her inner voice pleaded with her to act natural, a feat that seemed impossible considering the racing of her heart was making her hands tremble.

She could scream. No doubt her sisters would hear and come running. But then what? She would be putting them all in danger. No, better if she kept Jim talking until she could think of a plan…any plan.

She went up the porch steps, shoved her purse onto one of the wicker chairs, and tried desperately to force a natural-looking smile to her lips when she straightened. "I suppose I have a few minutes to spare. Let's go down to the shop and talk about what kind of painting you'd like me to do."

To her horror, she saw him move his hand to his pocket and pull out a gun. He kept it low, in front of his leg, out of sight of anyone who happened to see them from the shop. "I think we'll go in the house to discuss that, Mary."

He climbed the porch steps and made straight for her. Though she tried to stay calm, Mary couldn't help stumbling back. Rather than let him read the fear on her face, she spun around and reached for the door, but her hand fumbled nervously with the knob. Finally, she gave it a twist and pushed it open.

"Can I g-get you something to drink, Jim?" she stammered, leaving the door ajar as she stumbled toward the kitchen. When he didn't answer, she threw a glance at him over her shoulder.

He eyed her quizzically. "No, thank you. I don't need anything."

"Are you sure? We have lemonade."

He tilted his head at her and smiled, a slow and threatening sort of sneer that made her flesh crawl. "I thought you were in a hurry."

Mary stopped in the doorway to the kitchen. She could reach the knives, possibly, or dart for the back door, but she was no match for Jim in speed or strength, though obviously, it didn't matter, not with that gun in his hand. He paused at the entrance to the dining room, and Mary read the question in his gaze as he looked around. *Where did you put the teapot?*

Mary scrambled forward a step. "Perhaps we should talk in here." She motioned toward the kitchen. "Jim?"

If he heard her, he didn't show it. At last his head swiveled slowly toward her, and his eyes gleamed with a horrid mixture of excitement and greed. "You still have it, don't you?"

"Have what?" she whispered.

He shook his head and strolled leisurely toward her. "I know you have it. You told Della you did. And I would guess you have the painting too. Where is it?"

"What are you talking about?" She eased backward until her shoulders bumped the doorjamb.

"I think you know," he insisted quietly. "I think you're just now realizing how valuable those items of your uncle's are . . . but you most definitely *do* know what I'm talking about." His face hardened and his hand shot out to grip her arm, the other waving the gun wildly. "Where is the painting?"

Mary hissed in pain. "Someone stole it."

"Not *your* painting . . . the Nasmyth. When I saw that unique frame, I thought you'd been foolish enough to paint over it. Imagine my relief when I learned you'd only removed the original in order to reuse the frame." He frowned, and his grip on her arm tightened. "You didn't damage it, did you?"

Mary glanced down at the hand gripping her arm, noticing for the first time the paint under his fingernails. "The painting is safe and sound at the police station," she said through clenched teeth.

For a split second, Jim looked speechless—and then rage darkened his face, made his eyes wild. "Well, then we'll have to see about getting it back," he managed at last. Catching ahold of himself, he cleared his throat and narrowed his eyes to peer at her menacingly. "Look, Mary, I like you. I really would rather we took care of this business civilly." He let go of her arm and reached for his back pocket, pulling out his wallet. "I'll even pay you for the painting . . . assuming you throw in the teapot, of course."

"I'm not an idiot," Mary said, hoping he didn't hear the quiver in her voice. "I know the teapot is valuable."

He studied her for a moment and then slid the wallet back into his pocket. "That's too bad. It probably would have been better for you if you didn't know what the teapot was worth. As it is…I'm afraid I'm going to have to see to it that you have a rather untidy accident. Possibly your sisters too. And Della." He smiled amiably at her—as though they were discussing the weather.

Mary couldn't believe her ears. "Della? What have you done with her? Where is she?"

Shaking took hold of Mary's limbs, starting at her feet and running all the way through her to her fingertips. She couldn't back away. There was nowhere to go. It was then she saw a flash of red. Heard a thud. Saw a look of surprise flash across Jim's face. And then…

He crumpled to a heap on the floor.

CHAPTER THIRTY-ONE

Mary stared at Jim's prone body in disbelief. Martha stood over him, still wielding the wrought iron candlestick she had snatched off the hall table. Her eyes widened as she stared at it, then at Jim, and finally at Mary, who bent and picked up Jim's gun.

"Oh!" Backing up a step, she dropped the candlestick to the floor with a thud. "I've killed him."

As if to deny the charge, Jim groaned and stirred slightly.

"Well, he's not dead," Mary said, "but he's going to have one doozy of a headache when he comes to." She caught Martha's arm and pulled her aside. "C'mon, we'd better call the police before he wakes up."

Pounding footsteps sounded on the porch, and then Elizabeth and Rachel appeared, their eyes round as they stared at Jim sprawled on the hall floor.

"What happened? Are you all right?" they exclaimed almost at once.

Before she could reply, Officer Marks's car rumbled up the driveway. Mary stared in amazement. She'd been bluffing when she told Jim the police were on their way. She gaped at Elizabeth. "Did you call him?"

Elizabeth blew a stray lock of hair from her eyes, and she shook her head. "Not me."

"That was me," Martha said. Now that her breathing had returned to normal, a bit of the high color washed from her face. She drew a deep breath and wiped the sweat from her forehead.

Elizabeth hurried to let John in. Mary gave him the gun and explained how Jim had threatened her. "But, John, he has Della! You have to make him tell you where she is!" John and the others stared at her like she had two heads. "I don't think he's hurt her—not yet, anyway."

The three women watched as Jim was handcuffed and put in the back of John's police car. After a few minutes, John came back to the porch.

"You ladies will be happy to know that I've got a squad car and an ambulance on their way to Jim's apartment. That's where he's had Della stashed since he kidnapped her from her place last week. He says he hasn't mistreated her, except for keeping her tied up most of the time. I've asked the paramedics to check her out, and if she's okay, my officer will bring her here so I can get her story."

Mary's legs finally failed her, and she stumbled to a rocker and fell into it. Immediately Martha, Elizabeth, and Rachel stopped hugging, crying, and laughing and rushed to her. After a bit of fussing, a glass of water, and her share of the hugging and crying, Mary was able to string two words together.

"I was scared witless," she said, laughing shakily. "I've never been threatened like that before." She turned to Martha. "How did you know to show up when you did?"

Martha pointed to Rachel. "I knew you'd been to talk to Jim's grandfather, and ordinarily, you'd rush back to tell us what happened. When Rachel said she saw you talking on the porch with a man, I figured something out of the ordinary must be happening." She rubbed her eyes. "When I think of what might have happened..."

Rachel and Martha looked at each other, and Mary saw something silent pass between their raised eyebrows. They both went into the house. John looked at Mary, puzzled. "Where are they going?"

Mary smiled. "If I know Martha like I know Martha, she's thinking of how best to serve our guests. I'm thinking she and Rachel will be out here soon with sandwiches and cookies and lemonade."

Sure enough, about twenty minutes later, about the same time a squad car pulled up, Rachel came out with a tray of sandwiches and napkins, followed by Martha holding a tray of drinks. Hanging from her fingers under the tray was a basket of cookies.

But the trays and basket were hastily placed on the small table and forgotten when Della stepped out of the police car. All the women rushed to her, talking, laughing, and crying again, all trying to hug her at once.

"Hold on, now." John pulled a notepad from his pocket and clicked the top of his pen. "Let's get settled on the porch and hear Della's story while we eat. Della, you can start from the beginning, when you feel up to it."

"I'll explain everything," Della said, and put her hand to her head. "But I really do have to sit down. I'm feeling a bit dizzy after all the excitement."

John took Della's elbow and led her up the porch steps to a rocker. Elizabeth hurried to fetch her and the officer who brought her a sandwich and a glass of lemonade.

"Thank you." She took a sip, then looked squarely at John. "I suppose I should start by telling you why I didn't call the police when all this started."

At his nod, Della began unraveling the events of the past few days, starting with a phone call the day she sold the teapot to Mary and leading up to today. "I was just so frightened," she said. "Jim—well, I didn't know it was him at the time, of course—threatened to hurt me and anyone else who knew about the teapot. I couldn't tell him I'd already sold it to Mary, not without putting her in danger too. And then that evening, he came to the house and broke in through the veranda. He didn't believe me that I didn't have the teapot anymore. He tied me up and trashed my apartment looking for the teapot. When he didn't find it, he went through the apartment again, just to make more of a mess, and then he took me to his apartment. I've been there ever since."

"But how did he know where you live?" Martha asked.

"The same way he knew what she planned to do with the teapot. Facebook," Mary said.

Della frowned. "That can't be right. I don't have my address on my profile."

Mary thought a second and then smiled wryly. "Selma told him."

"Selma?" John looked from Mary to Della.

"Selma Mueller," Della said. "She advertised her garage sale in the paper. She used a photo of the teapot and several other items she had for sale. Jim must have seen the same ad."

"Which is why he went to her garage sale," Mary added. "Or maybe his grandfather saw the ad, and that's what got him started talking about the past."

"Jim overheard and went to the sale looking for the teapot, only to discover that Selma had already sold it," Martha said, snapping her fingers.

Mary nodded. "She said several people had been by asking about it. One of them had to have been Jim. Selma must have given him Della's name and address."

Della put down her uneaten sandwich. "If I've answered enough questions, I'd really like to go home now." She looked at John. "Would that be all right?"

"Yes, of course," John said. "We've got enough to charge Jim Olson, and we can get more details in the next few days, when you feel more up to it."

Mary put her hand to her cheek. "Della, your apartment is a mess. You can't go back there until it's cleaned up."

Della smiled at her. "You forget, Mary, I'm part of a fearsome foursome. One phone call, and the other three will be there with brooms and mops and cleaning rags." She stood and put her arm around Mary's shoulders. "You've got your sisters, and I've got mine. It's what family does."

Mary gave her a hug and watched as she walked to the car on the arm of the police officer. He helped her in, and with a final wave, drove off.

When Mary sat down again, Elizabeth said, "We know how he knew about the teapot. But what about the painting? How did he know about that? He never saw it."

"No, but I bet his grandfather did, and Jim saw the newspaper clippings his grandfather kept." Mary explained about the scraps of newspaper she'd seen when she went to visit Mr. Olson in the assisted living facility. "Jim claimed his grandfather liked to clip coupons, but I'd be willing to bet those were articles about the painting and possibly the teapot. I bet his grandfather kept them because they were about Paul. Jim saw them, which is how he got started looking for the items in the first place."

John nodded. "It's very likely there was something printed about them, since they were, in fact, stolen almost fifty years ago."

"You discovered something when you took the items back to the station?" Elizabeth asked.

"That's right. The teapot is part of a rare collection out of Belgium. The painting is by a famous Scottish artist named Patrick Nasmyth."

Mary sat up in her chair. "Nasmyth? That's the name Jim used."

He nodded. "Rare paintings like the one you gave me can be worth quite a bit, but overall, I think the real value was the total of *all* of the things that were stolen. All together, they're worth well over half a million dollars."

Mary sank against the back of her chair. "Uncle Paul stole over half a million dollars' worth of stuff?"

"It would appear so," John said, grimacing apologetically.

"We'll have to give John the note we found with the painting," Elizabeth said quietly, her expression pained.

"We'll have to finish looking through the boxes in the basement too, in case there are any more stolen items in with his things," Martha added, her words stilted with hurt.

"No wonder Daddy didn't want anyone in the family talking about him," Mary said sadly. Her heart cramped when she thought of what their father would say if he knew that the truth of Uncle Paul's past had finally been exposed.

"Daddy wasn't trying to cover it up," Elizabeth said, as though reading her thoughts. "All of this was just rumors back then. Maybe the reason Daddy forbade any mention of Uncle Paul was because he was hoping it would force him to repent. That's why the Amish shun their members."

"Maybe," Mary said, frowning doubtfully. "It still seems so unlike Mama and Daddy to be so unforgiving of someone. I mean, to bury him away from the family, to forbid the others from talking about him...I just can't believe that of them. It's so...harsh."

And how to explain the worn Bible they'd found in the basement, its pages tattered as if from use? There had to be more they still didn't understand. Deep down, she feared they never would.

CHAPTER THIRTY-TWO

Things seemed exceptionally quiet at the store now that Jim Olson was in custody. John was working with other law enforcement officials to return the stolen pieces to the rightful owners—or to the heirs of the rightful owners, to be exact. Mary sighed, thinking over what John had told them about the first owner passing away sometime in the nineties.

"Are you all right?" Martha slid the door closed on the baked goods and turned off the light in the display case. "You've been polishing that same mirror for almost ten minutes. You better get a move on if you want to close on time."

Mary glanced at the mirror. It was true. She couldn't get it any cleaner. She grimaced as she pushed it onto the shelf next to several other small, antique mirrors "You're right. Sorry. I just can't seem to get Uncle Paul out of my mind."

Martha's frown softened. "Me neither."

The bell above the door jangled, and both turned to see who was coming in. It was Rafe Porter.

Martha laid her tray down and glanced at Mary. "Uh-oh. I'll get him."

"No, that's all right." Mary held up her hand. "I'll go see what he wants. I've been meaning to talk to him anyway."

Martha's eyebrows rose, but she said nothing as Mary laid down her polishing cloth and wiped her hands nervously on her apron.

"I'll be right back." Lifting her chin, Mary strode toward Rafe and feigned more confidence than she could actually muster. "Good afternoon."

Rafe's lips split in *that* smile...the one she recognized because it was so similar to Brian's.

"Afternoon."

Though she wanted to slip her hands into her pockets, Mary forced them to hang casually at her sides. "What can I help you with today?"

"Oh, I'm just looking."

Mary took a deep breath. "Rafe, I want to apologize for not being as courteous to you as I should. The truth is, you remind me of someone who didn't treat me very well, and I shouldn't have projected that onto you. I hope you can forgive me."

Rafe's perfect smile slipped, and then he smiled again, a genuine smile she hadn't seen on him yet—one that reached his eyes. "I-I appreciate that, Mary. I hope we can start over and maybe become friends."

"I hope so too. We close in about five minutes, but feel free to holler if you see something you're interested in."

Rafe opened his mouth, but whatever he'd been about to say was cut short by Mary's direct but firm stare.

For the first time, a bit of the confidence seemed to seep from his shoulders. She even caught a glimmer of admiration in his eyes—and not the fake kind he put on when he was trying to charm the socks off a woman.

"I'll do that. Thank you, Mary."

"You're welcome."

Straightening her shoulders, Mary turned on her heel and went to the closet to grab the broom.

Oh, but it felt good to take her confidence back. Even better was the realization that it had belonged to her all along. More than likely, she would always have to deal with men like Rafe and Brian, but she didn't have to worry about that anymore. She recognized them now, and she knew the difference between them and men like—

Bill.

The bell jangled again and this time, Bill walked through. His sandy brown hair was disheveled, and he made it more so by running his fingers through it when he caught sight of her. He smelled of sawdust and hard work, which to Mary's mind was much better than any of the expensive fragrances she saw in stores.

She was surprised to feel her heart hitch as he leaned forward to rest his arms against the counter. "Hey."

"Hey yourself." She matched his posture and thought how glad she was that business was slow. "I'm surprised to see you. Are you looking for something?"

"Yep. You. I was hoping to catch the three of you before you started supper. I have something I need to show you and your sisters. Are you free for a bit?"

Mary was intrigued. She checked with Martha and Elizabeth, then came back to the counter. "They said to give us fifteen minutes, and we'll be ready to go."

"Sounds good. I'll wait at my truck."

Ten minutes later, the three sisters were climbing into Bill's truck. Mary and Martha sat in the back seat, and Elizabeth rode shotgun.

Mary swallowed a sudden knot in her throat and motioned toward the road. "So? Where are we heading?"

He glanced in her direction. "Um...let's just call it a surprise, okay?"

Why was he being so secretive?

Instead of pulling into town, Bill turned for the highway. He chatted the entire way, so Mary hardly noticed as the time went by. A short while later, however, they were pulling into the driveway of a house that looked familiar.

Mary's eyes widened as she stared through the windshield. "Frank and Selma Mueller?"

Bill's mouth curved in an uncertain smile as he turned on the seat to face them. "You remember the job I told you about? The woman who called for a bid on some modifications to her house because her husband was sick?"

He nodded toward the house.

Mary wiped her hands down her pant legs as she caught his meaning. "Okay...but what..."

"Go and talk to them. I think you'll want to hear what she and her husband have to say."

"Frank is here?" Elizabeth glanced toward the house and back. "I thought he was still in a nursing home."

"Uh-uh." Bill gestured toward a ramp that led toward the door. "I installed that yesterday. He came home today."

Though she still had doubts, Mary reached for the door handle. Before she slid from the seat, Bill turned to look at her.

"I'll be praying for you, okay?"

She nodded and slipped out of the truck, shutting the door behind her.

The front door to the Muellers' house opened as she approached, and Selma beckoned them forward.

Her mouth dry, Mary managed a small, "Hello."

"Hello, Mary, Elizabeth, Martha. Thank you for coming." Selma opened the door wide. "Please come in."

Once again, Selma led them to the parlor off the main hall. This time, Frank waited there. He still had his oxygen tank, but his color looked better, and he smiled as he looked up at their entrance.

"Hello, Mr. Mueller," Elizabeth said. "You're looking well. I'm glad to see you're back home."

He gave a low chuckle. "You and me both. And please, call me Frank. Have a seat."

Mary eased onto the couch, and Martha and Elizabeth sank down on either side of her. Certain her confusion showed on her face, she looked back and forth between the Muellers. "I'm sorry...I'm not sure what all this is about."

Selma motioned toward her husband. "Tell them, Frank."

He swallowed hard, his Adam's apple bobbing in his thin neck. "Yes, I suppose it's best if we get right to it."

Despite his words, he hesitated, his hands shaking as he clasped them tightly in his lap. Finally, he drew a breath and looked up at them. "I heard about Jim Olson. I understand he's been taken into custody?"

"That's correct. But how—?"

"One of the benefits of living in a small town," Selma said with an awkward smile. "Everyone knows everyone else's business."

"Oh. Right." Mary held herself stiffly, waiting.

"One of the other 'benefits' as my wife called it," Frank continued, "is that people talk. The problem is, they don't always get it right. And this time around, I'd like to help set the record straight."

"Go on," Martha urged.

Mary braced herself for whatever words he would utter next.

Frank leaned forward to grip the arms of his chair. "After everything that's happened, you probably think your uncle was a thief. Am I right?"

He didn't wait for any of them to answer, but forged ahead.

"Well, that's not true. I wasn't exactly straight with you all when you came to see me at the nursing home. I'm sorry for that, but I hope you believe that I was only trying to keep a promise I made to your uncle many, many years ago."

"What promise was that?" Mary rasped, her throat dry.

Frank sighed heavily. Selma leaned toward him in concern, but he waved her back and trained his gaze on Mary. "It all happened a long time ago. Paul had gotten mixed up with the wrong crowd. If you've been investigating, you probably already know that."

She nodded.

"Well, a couple of those fellows he was running around with got it into their heads to make some money quick. They'd heard that a wealthy family nearby was going out of town and thought it might be a good idea to break into their house and steal some of their stuff. Your uncle was against it, but hard as he tried, he couldn't talk those boys out of it."

Mary's heart had begun to race. She spared a glance at Selma, who was watching her husband anxiously.

Elizabeth leaned forward. "Uncle Paul told you all of this?"

Here, Frank's face fell, and he looked at his wife, who nodded for him to continue.

"He didn't have to," Frank said. "*I* was one of those fellows trying to talk him into it."

Confusion thundered in Mary's head. "Wait…so you're telling me you and Uncle Paul stole the stuff we found?"

"Not me. I would have," he added quickly, "if your uncle hadn't stopped me, but Paul refused to let me go with them. If it wasn't for him, we'd probably all have landed in jail."

Mary pondered this a moment and then blew out a breath. "So, what happened?"

Frank spoke slowly at first, but as he continued, his voice grew stronger and his words came faster.

"The night the break-in was supposed to happen, Paul came to talk to me. He pleaded with me to think about my wife and what would happen to her if we got caught. Normally, I'd have been too hardheaded to listen, but for some reason, that night he got through. I agreed to stay behind."

"But he went through with the robbery?" Martha asked.

Frank shook his head vehemently. "No. He talked to—" He stopped and licked his lips. "The other guy is long gone now. It would only hurt his family for me to involve him by speaking his name." He sucked in a deep breath and blew it out. "Paul went to the other guy and begged him to reconsider. He wouldn't listen, even after Paul refused to go with him."

"But...if he didn't go, how did he end up with the stuff?" Elizabeth asked.

"After the break-in, the other guy got cold feet. He knew if he tried to pawn off the stuff he'd stolen, he'd be caught. He gave the stuff to Paul—well, almost all of it."

"And Paul brought it to you."

"That's right. I think he was afraid his family would find out if he tried to leave the stuff at his place." Frank's eyes grew damp as he reached absently for his wife's hand. "Your uncle was a good man, Mary. He saved my marriage, especially once the rumors started. He never breathed a word to anyone, not even Selma."

The rumors! Mary's throat tightened as she thought about what Uncle Paul's silence had cost him.

"Why—" The muscles in her neck tightened. She drew a breath and started again. "Why didn't he take the stolen items to the police?"

"He intended to. I believe that beyond a doubt. I think he was trying to find a way to do it without implicating me or anyone else. And people kept on thinking he was involved in the theft, because of the crowd he ran with, and because he wouldn't talk about it. But then the accident happened, and he never got the chance to return the items. It's easy to blame a dead man who can't defend himself."

"So, you *didn't* forget about the items in your attic," Martha said, her tone accusing.

Frank shook his head slowly. "I couldn't, no matter how hard I tried."

Mary searched his face and found only brokenness and regret. After a long moment, she said, "I believe you." She looked at her sisters, and they nodded in agreement.

Frank's shoulders slumped.

"But there are two things I don't understand."

Both Selma and Frank looked at her.

"We found a note—it was written on a napkin. It said 'Target ready. Don't get caught.' The letters we compared them to in Uncle Paul's Bible were written in the same hand. And there was a map. We figure it let the thief know which house to rob. If Uncle Paul didn't write the note and draw the map, who did?"

Frank smiled sadly. "We all attended the same school, the one on the Old Philadelphia Pike."

"Weavertown."

He nodded. "Handwriting was important in those days. Everyone had to learn to write their letters neatly. And uniformly."

Understanding dawned, and with it an incredible sense of relief. "So he didn't write the note? And he didn't draw the map either?" Mary asked.

Frank hesitated for several long, drawn-out seconds and then finally crossed his arms over his chest. "If you don't mind...I really would rather not say."

Mary took a deep breath. This question was more difficult. The answer could incriminate Uncle Paul again. "The second thing I don't understand. If Uncle Paul brought the stolen items to you, how did the painting end up in our basement? Did he bring the painting to you or not?"

Frank frowned at her. "There was a painting?"

Mary looked at Elizabeth and Martha and saw the dread on their faces. It was reflected in her own face, she knew. "There was a painting in a crate in our basement. That's where we found the note and the map. The painting is a famous one, worth a lot of money, and the police think it came from the same heist as the teapot."

Frank continued to look puzzled for a few moments, and then his face smoothed out as realization dawned. "Ah! That must be—remember, I said that my friend brought *almost* all of the items to Paul? Later he told me that he hadn't given everything to Paul right away. He'd made Paul think he had, but he kept one item and toyed with the idea of selling it. In the end he ended up taking that to Paul also. But it was after Paul had brought the other things to me. Later Paul told me he was going to bring one more item...but he never got the chance. That must have been the painting."

Elizabeth and Mary stood, relief written all over them. Mary pushed to her feet, suddenly feeling much lighter than she had when she walked into the Muellers' home.

"Thank you so much for telling us what happened, Mr. Mueller," she said, saddened to see the fear reflected in his eyes, and the tears glinting in his wife's.

Selma rose too, and looked from the sisters to her husband and back. "If you don't mind me asking, what will you do with this information?"

Martha buttoned her jacket. "The stolen property we have has been returned, or will be once we go through the rest of Uncle Paul's things. If you still have the cufflinks and pocket watch or anything else from the theft, you need to give those to the police also. From what I've learned about Uncle Paul, I don't think he would want us to press any further than that."

Selma exhaled in a rush, and her shoulders bent as though she'd been holding them upright through sheer force of will.

Mary's gaze drifted to the window and the pickup truck parked outside. "Does Bill know?"

Both Frank and Selma shook their heads.

"All we told him is that we needed to talk to you all," Selma said. "He said he'd take care of the rest."

The ride back home was quiet. Mary knew Bill was wondering why Frank and Selma had wanted to see them, but she also knew he would patiently wait until she was ready to tell him. When they pulled into the driveway, Martha broke the silence.

"Bill, we appreciate what you've done today. I was thinking, maybe you could come for dinner tomorrow night, and we could explain everything to you?"

Tears filled Mary's eyes, and she was once again grateful for Martha's thoughtfulness. Elizabeth echoed her invitation, and Bill said he'd be happy to come. After Mary climbed out of the truck, she reached through his open window and put her hand on his shoulder. "You're a good friend, Bill Richmond."

He gave her a smile, reached up, and squeezed her fingers. Then, with a little wave, he drove out of the driveway and off down the road.

CHAPTER THIRTY-THREE

As the sisters walked through the front door, Mary's cell phone rang, startling them all. She pulled it from her pocket, and her eyes grew wide as she stared at the number. "It's Uncle George."

"Answer it," Martha urged with a wave of her hands.

Mary hit ANSWER and the SPEAKER button almost simultaneously. "Hello, Uncle George."

Elizabeth and Martha crowded in close.

"Hello, Mary. I got your messages. I'm so sorry I missed you. I've been traveling and just got home last night. I dropped my cell phone last week and haven't gotten around to replacing it yet. I hope everything's all right at the farm."

"The farm is fine, Uncle George," she assured him quickly. She looked to her sisters for support. Then she took a breath and continued. "Listen, Elizabeth and Martha are here with me. If you don't mind, we need to ask you a couple of questions. Unfortunately, it may be a bit upsetting to you, so I apologize in advance."

Uncle George didn't speak for a moment. Mary held her breath, waiting. Uncle George had always been the most somber member of the family, perhaps because he was the oldest.

To her surprise, he let out a long sigh and said, "I wondered when one of you would try to get in touch."

Mary blinked, and her gaze shot to Martha and then Elizabeth. "Wh-what?"

"To be honest, I've been expecting your call."

"But...how can that be?" Martha cut in before Mary could ask. "You know what this is about?"

Again, he hesitated. "I'm afraid I do, Martha. I know exactly what this is about. And I think it's time you girls knew the truth."

CHAPTER THIRTY-FOUR

I don't understand. How could you possibly know why we were trying to reach you?" Martha pressed, taking the phone from Mary and holding it close to her mouth.

"Gertrude called and said you had been asking questions about Paul," he explained. "Though even if she hadn't, I knew it would only be a matter of time before the three of you stumbled on the things in the basement."

Mary stopped pacing and spun. "Wait, you mean you knew about the painting?"

"Painting?" Static cut through the line for a brief instant, and then Uncle George returned. "What painting?"

"Uncle Paul's painting, the one we found in the basement with some of his things." She moved closer, as though a few steps could lessen the miles separating them.

"I'm sorry, Mary, I don't know anything about that. I just figured you girls would happen on his things and be curious."

She met her sisters' gazes. Martha stuck the phone out toward her. Mary took it, her palms damp with sweat. "Uncle George, we know that Mama and Daddy thought Paul was involved in a burglary, and that they practically disowned him because of it. We know that's why they wouldn't even let him be buried in the family plot. We know what caused the rift in our family—we just don't know how Mama and Daddy could treat him that way." She could barely choke out the words through her tears. "It's so unfair. Uncle Paul didn't steal those things. He was innocent, and even if he wasn't, how could they—"

"Mary, honey, please. Calm down." Uncle George's voice was as she remembered him. Kind, unhurried, soothing. "Is that what you all think? That your parents disowned Paul because they believed he was a thief?" He groaned. "Sweetheart, that's not what happened. Your mother and daddy knew Paul was innocent. They knew he was a little wild sometimes, and had the wrong friends, but they knew he wasn't a liar or a thief."

Mary stared through her tears at her sisters and saw the tears on their faces. She also saw the relief and hope in their eyes. Their mother and father were who they'd believed them to be—forgiving, loyal, compassionate.

Martha wiped her eyes. "But Uncle George, what happened? Why isn't Paul buried with the rest of the family?"

They could hear Uncle George's heavy sigh across the miles. "Because he grew up a conservative Mennonite, and he joined the navy. He wanted to see the world. He joined up without even graduating from high school. Served eight years, came home from Vietnam. Then the whole kerfuffle happened with the burglary, and then his accident. The pastor of our church in those days was very strict and wouldn't allow Paul to be buried with the family. He wasn't able to get your grandparents and parents to disown Paul while he was alive, but they didn't have any control over the cemetery rules. Pastor Beinbreck was unyielding."

Martha looked puzzled. "How come no one we asked told us that Paul had joined the navy? Didn't they know?"

"They couldn't have known," said Uncle George. "When he left, all we told people was that he left to travel the world. The only one outside the immediate family who knew was Pastor Beinbreck, and in the end, we regretted telling him."

Elizabeth too was wiping her eyes. "That's why there were no pictures of him in Grandma Lois's photo album past his junior year in high school. He wasn't here." She moved closer to the phone. "But Uncle George, why did Daddy forbid you all to talk about him to us?"

Uncle George cleared his throat. "Um...you have a couple of aunts...I won't say which ones...who weren't quite as charitable to Paul as your mother and father were," he said. "Your father didn't want them to poison your minds against Paul."

Mary exchanged glances with Martha and Elizabeth. She knew they were thinking of the same aunts as she was.

"But you need to know, girls, that your grandmother Lois wrote Paul every week he was in the navy, no matter where he was. And your father made sure he got Christmas and birthday presents every year." Mary heard someone in the background, then Uncle George spoke again. "I have to go, girls. You all take care, and I hope we get to see each other real soon."

They said their goodbyes, and Mary put her phone back in her pocket. Martha and Elizabeth went into the kitchen. Mary followed them, knowing the feelings running through each of them were too deep for words. She was remembering what Rachel's grandmother had said about how Paul had changed when he came back. Her heart broke, thinking of him struggling alone to recover from the war in Vietnam.

While Elizabeth took fixings for sandwiches from the fridge and Martha made lemonade, Mary went to the cupboard to get plates to set the table. Suddenly Martha broke the silence. "Mary, I was hoping that maybe we can get your picture back from the police. If they find it in Jim's apartment, that is."

Elizabeth looked up from slicing tomatoes. "Oh, I hope they find it. I want us to hang it where we can see it every day."

Mary's heart warmed at her sisters' words. "I'm afraid it might be damaged. Jim said something about thinking I painted over the Nasmyth, so I'm afraid he might have rubbed off some of the paint. I won't know if I can salvage it until I see it."

"Well, if you can, I think Elizabeth is right," Martha said. "I'd like to be reminded every day of Mama and Daddy's love for Uncle Paul, and how compassion is better than judgment."

"I've also been thinking of something else," Mary said slowly, looking Elizabeth and then Martha in the eyes. "Do you think it would be possible to move Uncle Paul's grave? Don't you think it's time he joined the rest of the family?"

Elizabeth's eyes widened. "Mary, that's a splendid idea," she said. "I'll ask John about what we'd have to do to make that happen."

When all was set, and they were sitting in their places, Mary took her sisters' hands. As she bowed her head for grace, she once again thought of her favorite etching in the shop: "I thank God for protecting me from what I thought I wanted and blessing me with what I didn't know I needed." This is what she needed. Friends like Rachel and Bill, who helped clear up the mysteries in her life. Even a friend like Rafe, who made her stand up for herself. The sweet memories in every wall of this house, echoing with compassion, forgiveness, joy, and love. And the two hands she was holding. Especially these two extraordinary women—sisters in blood, in love, in heart.

A NOTE FROM THE AUTHOR

Irving Berlin wrote a wonderful song about sisters. In fact, I'm humming it now as I type, and thinking about the four wonderful, devoted, strong women I call sisters. Like the characters Mary, Martha, and Elizabeth, each of my sisters is special, with different strengths and weaknesses to set her apart. One is creative, like Mary. Another is organized and efficient, like Martha. All are loving and devoted to family. More than anything, I wanted that bond to be a strong theme throughout this book. My mother told me once that people would come and go, but family would be with me forever. As with most things, I have learned how right she was. My sisters have cheered me from the sidelines from the day I sold my first book. They have prayed for me, cried with me, and laughed with me over some really bad jokes. I think that's why it was such a pleasure writing about the relationship between the Classen sisters. With each scene, I appreciated my sweet, beautiful sisters more. I hope those of you with siblings do as well.

Elizabeth Ludwig

ABOUT THE AUTHOR

Elizabeth Ludwig is an accomplished speaker and teacher, often attending conferences where she lectures on editing for fiction writers, crafting effective novel proposals, and conducting successful editor/agent interviews. Book three in her popular Edge of Freedom series, *Tide and Tempest*, was named a finalist for the Gayle Wilson Award of Excellence. Elizabeth was also named a finalist in the 2015 Selah Awards for her novella "One Holy Night," part of the best-selling anthology collection, *Christmas Comes to Bethlehem, Maine*. Most recently, she was honored to be awarded a HOLT Medallion for her book, *A Tempting Taste of Mystery*, part of the Sugarcreek Amish Mysteries series from Guideposts. Her latest releases include *Shifting Sands* and *Sheeps Passing in the Night*, part of the Mysteries of Martha's Vineyard series, also from Guideposts. To learn more, visit ElizabethLudwig.com.

BARN FINDS

I stumbled across an interesting article recently about an eleven-year-old boy with an interest in antiques. This real-life "picker," as people who are skilled in the art of buying antiques and then selling them for profit are called, found his fifteen minutes of fame when he bought a spoon from a local flea market. Crafted by Chief John Robson, a noted carver of totem poles in the late 1800s, the spoon turned out to be quite valuable. A drawing in Robson's sketchbook proved the authenticity of the find, capturing the attention of networks and celebrity pickers alike. While it is unlikely that another spoon exactly like the one the boy purchased would be found in the Classen family barn, it is fun to think that something by Chief Robson could turn up there, and some clever young picker would be wise enough to snatch it up.

FRESH FROM MARTHA'S KITCHEN

Roasted Chicken with Asparagus and Garlic Potatoes

Ingredients

1 pound Yukon Gold potatoes, cut into one-inch pieces

1 head garlic, cloves separated and peeled

3 tablespoons extra-virgin olive oil, divided

Kosher salt and freshly ground pepper

4 skinless, boneless chicken breasts (about six ounces each)

1 bunch medium asparagus (about one pound), trimmed and halved

1 pint grape tomatoes

½ cup grated parmesan cheese (about one ounce)

¼ cup chopped fresh parsley

2 teaspoons finely grated lemon zest

Directions

Put rimmed baking sheet on lowest oven rack and preheat to 425 degrees. Toss potatoes and garlic cloves with one tablespoon olive oil, ¼ teaspoon salt, and a few grinds pepper in a bowl; set aside. Season chicken with ½ teaspoon salt and a few grinds pepper. Heat 1 tablespoon olive oil in large skillet over medium heat. Add chicken; cook until browned, approximately 2 minutes per side. Transfer to hot baking sheet. Scatter potatoes and garlic around chicken; reserve bowl. Bake until chicken is just cooked through, about 5 minutes. Transfer chicken to a plate and tent with foil; leave potatoes and garlic on baking sheet. Add asparagus and tomatoes to reserved bowl; toss with remaining 1 tablespoon olive oil and ¼ teaspoon salt. Add to baking sheet with potatoes. Bake until vegetables are tender and tomatoes start to burst, 13 to 15 minutes. Remove baking sheet from oven; switch oven to broil. Toss parmesan, parsley, and lemon zest in small bowl. Nestle chicken in vegetables and sprinkle everything with parmesan mixture. Broil until golden, 1 to 2 minutes.

Read on for a sneak peek of another exciting book
in the Mysteries of Lancaster County series!

An Unbroken Circle
by Tricia Goyer and Cara Putman

The morning sun was nearing its zenith as Martha Classen Watts steered her car into the drive leading to her family home. A warm sense of satisfaction filled her when she saw at least a dozen cars and half as many buggies parked in front of the large barn that housed the combination thrift store and gift shop she and her two sisters had reopened ten or twelve weeks ago. Who would have guessed that after Mama's funeral she and her younger sister, Mary, would move back to Bird-in-Hand to live with their older sister, Elizabeth, in their childhood home and run Secondhand Blessings together? Martha liked to think the store was as popular now as it was when their grandparents started the business way back in the 1930s.

She gathered her handbag from the passenger seat and opened the door. A moment later, she stepped out of the car and then shifted to close the door. When she turned back to the red barn, Elizabeth was waiting for her.

"How was your trip into town?" she asked. "You had quite a few errands to run."

Martha nodded. "I got most everything done I needed to." And she had stayed busy. She didn't expect her sisters to remember, but two weeks from today would mark the second anniversary of Chuck's death. Becoming a widow at age fifty-three wasn't something she'd ever even contemplated, and some days it was harder to find joy than others.

She brought her thoughts back to the present. "Did we have many customers this morning?"

"Considering we've only been open an hour? Good enough."

Martha glanced at her watch. Was it really only eleven thirty? "You mean an hour and a half."

"I do." Elizabeth grinned and linked arms with Martha. The two walked to the store together, Elizabeth's khaki skirt brushing against Martha's leg.

The barn was built of wood planks painted a bright red. The building was open with a few items displayed on the wide door. Martha saw Mary sitting in one of the chairs in the small conversation nook the sisters had added to the shop. An Amish woman sat next to her, and the two were embroiled in a conversation.

Martha looked around the store's interior, and her heart sank as she realized little, if anything, from the detailed checklist she had written up had been accomplished. "You saw the list I pinned on the bulletin board in the office, right?"

Elizabeth nodded as she stepped away from Martha and shifted knickknacks around a table. "Of course. You only mentioned it five times at breakfast."

"And you got through the list?"

"I didn't say that. We've had a busy morning, as you can see."

Martha glanced around the interior. Handcrafted and antique furniture filled Elizabeth's favorite part of the store.

Mary liked the children's area the best, with its bright colors and toys. The other sections included household goods, books, crafts, decorative items, tools, and jewelry, all displayed on beautiful Amish-made shelving. Clothing racks with gently used and vintage adult and children's clothing rounded out the eclectic atmosphere of Secondhand Blessings. Near the checkout counter and along one wall was Martha's display case, filled with scones, breads, cookies, muffins, and seasonal delights like jams, honey, and maple syrup. This addition to the thrift store inventory had been a hit. Once people tasted her marvelous cooking, they returned for more.

Martha tried to see the displays as customers walking in the door would, and what she saw made her fingers itch to get busy. Spring was fully behind them now, and June meant all things summer. Yet even though she'd left a to-do list that included updating their seasonal displays, there was Mary being Mary, sitting down and having what looked like a leisurely conversation with an elderly Amish woman. While she loved Mary, sometimes her younger sister's proclivity to sit and chat when there was work to be done could drive Martha crazy.

So much had to happen to make this endeavor a permanent part of their worlds. As Elizabeth left and came back in with the mail and a couple of packages, Martha sighed. At least her older sister was willing to be part of making Secondhand Blessings work. Martha moved to the table farthest from Mary and the Amish woman whom she could now see was Betty Yoder. Martha set to work straightening the table's contents. It might take a little creativity, but as she sifted through the accessories on the table, she began to see a summer theme emerge.

After the table was organized, Martha noted Betty had stood and was straightening her bonnet and smoothing her apron. Then she followed Mary to the counter, where Elizabeth had just finished ringing up a customer. Betty held a quilt in her hands, and as Martha looked closer, she recognized it. The quilt was one that Anne Hostetler had shown interest in yesterday. Martha had all but promised Anne to hold it for her for a couple of days until Anne could figure out if she could afford it or not. In retrospect, maybe that hadn't been the best thing to do. Martha set down the teapot she'd been holding and hurried after Betty and Mary.

"I'm sorry, Betty, but I have an interested buyer in that quilt already." She turned to Mary. "Didn't you see the note I put beside it?"

"There wasn't a note, Martha." Mary stroked the quilt.

Elizabeth frowned. "Martha, you should have put it under the counter or in the back if it wasn't for sale."

"Yes, I can see that now. Well, that was my mistake, not Anne's, so I feel obligated to keep my word to her. She was so delighted to find it here."

One of Betty's eyebrows lifted, and she sniffed. "What did you promise this other customer? Mary here just promised it to me."

"I promised her I would hold it until tomorrow," Martha said. She touched Mary's arm. "You remember Anne Hostetler, Mama's friend, don't you? I can't go back on my word to her." She gently took the quilt from Betty and set it on the counter. "I'm sorry to disappoint you, but this one isn't available. I'll be glad to find you a similar one."

Betty's chin jutted. "Not good enough. This is the quilt I want." She folded her thin arms across her chest. "The quilt belongs to me, so you will have to call Anne Hostetler and tell her the quilt is sold. I do not want anyone else to have it, and especially not *her*."

Martha's eyes met Mary's, and questions filled her sister's gaze. Why was Betty acting this way, especially about Anne? Since Anne had been one of Mama's best friends, the three sisters had spent a lot of time with Anne, and she'd always been pleasant and kind. Obviously, Betty Yoder didn't view her that way. Martha was a bit taken back by the Amish woman's open display of criticism.

"Betty, I can't do that." Martha fought the urge to mirror Betty's antagonistic posture. "I promised to hold it for her."

The defiance in the woman's eyes softened, replaced by a pleading look. "That quilt belonged to my family years ago. It was my *aenti* Melinda's. She never married and lived with my *dawdiss* until their deaths. As a child, I stayed at their home. I remember waking up and reading the scriptures on the quilt as the morning light beamed through the window." She smiled at the memory. "I loved running my fingers along the words, and before I knew it I'd memorized many of the verses. At some point the quilt disappeared, and I did not know what happened to it until now."

Elizabeth ran her hand over the quilt. "What makes you so sure this is that quilt, the one your aunt owned?"

"The verses are the same."

Martha took a closer look at the quilt. It was a crazy quilt, a random assortment of mismatched blocks that had various

Bible verses embroidered on them. The blocks weren't the normal precise geometric blocks that were more common in the beautiful Amish quilts in the shops in Bird-in-Hand. Instead, it was a chaotic blend of different fabrics and styles of embroidery, each with a different Bible verse. The chaotic nature of the quilt actually added to its charm.

Mary appealed to Elizabeth. "Couldn't we at least talk to Anne about it? If the quilt was in Betty's family, maybe we should let her buy it."

Martha looked at Mary. "But Anne should still have first choice."

Mary's expression didn't waver. "Please."

Elizabeth looked from one sister to the other and then sighed. "All right. We can talk to Anne." She turned to Betty. "We can't make any promises about what she'll say."

"Thank you." Betty turned to leave. "Please let me know as soon as possible."

Martha sighed. "I'll get back to you as soon as I can, Betty." There was so much to do, but she would make time to call Anne. And when Anne said she still wanted the quilt, as Martha expected her to, this little tug-of-war would be over. The moment Betty exited the barn's door, Mary turned to Martha. "We have to get Anne to let us sell the quilt to Betty."

"Why?"

"Because it's a matter of heritage. If this quilt was Betty's aunt Melinda's, then we need to let her buy it. Maybe we should even let her have it."

"Mary." Martha shook her head. "We sell secondhand items. By definition, all those items belonged to someone already. If we start giving away items because they were once in someone's family, we'll never make a profit."

Elizabeth stepped between them. "How about I call Anne and see what she thinks. Surely if I explain everything to her, she'll decide to let Betty have the quilt." Elizabeth picked up the phone and dialed Anne's number. When Anne answered, Elizabeth moved to the corner to keep their conversation private. Martha knew Elizabeth would never do anything to embarrass Anne or make her feel as if the sisters were ganging up on her.

It was only a minute before Elizabeth put the phone down and walked back over to them, a frown marring her delicate features. "There's a problem, and I'm afraid Betty's mistaken. Anne says the quilt actually belonged to *her* family. She told me her cousin Irma made it. She also told me that she's not surprised that Betty would say otherwise."

How could two women have such a strong connection with the same quilt? Was one of them mistaken, or lying, about their connection to the piece? If so, which one, and why?